CLUTCHING THE STEEL HANDLE OF THE BUCKET, I WALKED QUICKLY TOWARD THE GREENHOUSE SINK, WANTING TO GET THE WATER AND GET OUT OF THERE. . . .

*b*ut when I reached for the faucet, I stopped. On the shelf above the sink sat a jade plant, its fleshy almond-shaped leaves glimmering in the moonlight. It moved. I took a step back, staring at it, knowing it was impossible, but certain I had seen it. The branches had moved, as if invisible fingers had riffled them.

I was going crazy. I was seeing what my mother had seen before she died, things knotting, things moving. *"There's no hand touching them, baby. They move by themselves."* Maybe Aunt Jule was right: I was obsessed with my mother, so much so that I was imagining her experiences.

I fought the panic rising in me and reached for the faucet again, turning the handle hard. When the bucket was half full, I shut off the stream.

I thought I felt a trickle on my neck—spray from the faucet or my own sweat. Reaching up to wipe it, I touched dry skin and my necklace. It wasn't water, but the chain creeping along my neck. I looked down at the silver heart, rising like a slow tide, moving closer and closer to my throat. I dropped the bucket and spun around, as if to catch someone pulling the necklace, but no one was there. I clawed at the chain, grabbing it before it could choke me . . .

Dark Secrets: Legacy of Lies
Dark Secrets: Don't Tell

Available from Archway Paperbacks

DARK SECRETS
Don't Tell

Elizabeth Chandler

AN ARCHWAY PAPERBACK
Published by POCKET BOOKS
New York   London   Toronto   Sydney   Singapore

This book is a work of fiction. Names, characters, places and incidents are products of the author's imagination or are used fictitiously. Any resemblance to actual events or locales or persons, living or dead, is entirely coincidental.

AN ARCHWAY PAPERBACK *Original*

An Archway Paperback published by
POCKET BOOKS, a division of Simon & Schuster, Inc.
1230 Avenue of the Americas, New York, NY 10020

ISBN: 0-7434-0029-1

First Archway Paperback printing March 2001

10 9 8 7 6 5 4 3

DARK SECRETS is a trademark of Simon & Schuster, Inc.

AN ARCHWAY PAPERBACK and colophon are registered trademarks of Simon & Schuster, Inc.

Front cover illustration by Sandy Young/Studio Y

Printed in the U.S.A.

IL 6+

To Bob,

You're the best!
Love you.

one

The screen door creaked open. I shut my eyes, hoping Mommy would think I was asleep and go away. I wanted to burrow under my bedsheets, but I lay as still as I could, hardly breathing.

"I can't sleep, Lauren."

I sat up. "Nora! Next time, say it's you."

She stood by my bed, looking like a skinny ghost in her pale cotton nightie.

"Someone keeps whispering. And Bunny is missing. I can't sleep," she said.

Bunny was a stuffed animal with fur worn flat as Aunt Jule's washcloths. Though Nora was twelve, two years older than I, she still took Bunny everywhere.

"I think he's on the dock. Want me to get him?"

Nora was afraid of water, this summer even more than last.

"No, I can go as far as the dock," she replied, then left my bedroom the way she had come, through the door to the upper porch.

I lay down, soothed by the sound of a sailboat line clanging against a mast. I came here every summer and loved Aunt Jule's big wooden house with its long double porches, the old boathouse on the river, and the overgrown gardens. Every year, as far back as I could remember, I came to play with my godmother's children, Nora and Holly, and their friend Nick.

Nick and Holly, a year older than I, had taught me all kinds of stuff Mommy didn't like. Aunt Jule never minded. She took care of us the way she took care of her house and garden—trusting somehow that we'd all survive. Being a kid was easy here in Wisteria.

But not this summer. Mommy had come, and she and Aunt Jule were fighting. It got worse at night, especially if Mommy drank wine. Afterward I would hear her walking the porches up and down, up and down. Sometimes she'd come into my room to talk to me.

"Someone has been in my room, baby," she'd say. "Someone has tied knots in all my scarves and necklaces. Someone hates me."

It scared me when she talked like that. When we were back in Washington, she often feared that people were following us. It was just reporters and photographers who wanted a picture of the famous senator's wife and daughter. I got used to it, but Mommy got more and more frightened by them. I thought it would be better at Aunt Jule's, but it wasn't.

She'd tell me things were moving in her room. "There's no hand touching them, baby. They move by themselves."

After a while she'd fall asleep, curled up on my bed. I'd lie awake for a long time, and when I finally closed my eyes, I'd dream of things moving with no hand touching them. In my dreams people chased us and tried to choke us with scarves and necklaces.

But Mommy hadn't come tonight, not yet. Maybe I'd fall asleep and feel safe and happy the way I used to at Aunt Jule's. The mist on the river was thick tonight, like a big soft comforter laid over the water, the edge of it lapping the house. I sank down in its friendly darkness, closed my eyes, and dreamed of playing treasure hunt with Nick.

In my dream the clank of a line against a sailboat mast became louder until it sounded like a bell being rung. The ringing wouldn't stop. I sat up suddenly. It was the dock bell—the big bell we were supposed to ring if there was trouble on the river.

"Nora!" I cried, then jumped out of bed and ran to the porch outside my room.

Holly, whose bedroom was next to mine, hurried out at the same time.

"Nora went down to the dock," I told her, panicky.

A light went on downstairs, cutting a path of white through the mist. Aunt Jule ran across the lawn toward the water, her bathrobe billowing behind her like a cape. Holly and I rushed to the end of the long porch and raced down the outside stairs.

The heavy mist blotted out the river and the dock. We paused for a moment at the top of the hill, straining to see, then ran down the grassy slope. I stepped on something sharp. Holly heard my cry and turned around. "It's okay. Okay," I told her, waving her on.

Close to the river edge she stopped and bent over. As I got nearer, I saw that Nora was safe, huddled on the ground.

"Where's Mother?" Holly asked her sister when I had caught up.

Nora pointed toward the water, her hand shaking.

Aunt Jule's voice sounded strange in the heavy mist, as if it were separate from her. "Holly, call 911."

Holly turned to me. "Lauren, go call."

"You run faster," I argued. "And you're wearing shoes."

"Go, Holly!" her mother shouted. She was wading in from the dark river, carrying something. I watched the way she swayed from side to side, as if the burden were heavy. I started into the water.

"Stay there, Lauren. Get back on shore."

I backed up onto the dry land, but away from the whimpering Nora, my stomach in a knot. I could tell from Aunt Jule's voice that something was wrong. The bundle she was carrying was long and limp. Even before I could see her clearly, I knew it was my mother. When Aunt Jule reached me, she laid her down in the grass. My mother's dark eyes stared up at me.

"Mommy?" I said softly. "Mommy? Mommy!" I cried. I picked up her hand and shook it.

Aunt Jule caught my wrist. "She—she can't hear you, love," she said, then closed my mother's eyes.

two

The grief counselor had said I would go back to Wisteria when I was ready. It took me seven years.

Sunday afternoon, as I stood at the top of High Street in one of the prettiest river towns on Maryland's Eastern Shore, I wondered why I had stayed away so long. Wisteria was not only the home of the godmother I loved, but the place where I was born. It was the summertime kingdom in which I had been allowed to run safe and free.

I walked down the sidewalk, enjoying the familiar feel of bumpy brick, hot beneath my sandals. Pots of red geraniums sat on broad steps. Impatiens tumbled over baskets hanging from painted wood porches. The Colonial Days Festival, held every June, was in full swing, and people crowded into shops like Urschpruk's Books. In front of Faye's Gallery wind chimes hung as they always had in one of the sycamores lining the main street.

Then the wind shifted. I smelled the river. Everything went cold inside me. Despite the sunlight, I started to shiver. For a moment I thought of returning to my car and driving straight back to Birch Hill Academy. This was why I hadn't come back here. This was why boarding with teachers and vacationing with my father and his political staff had seemed the better way to spend a summer.

I forced myself to keep walking and tried to focus on the present, making it a game to identify everything that was different: the new sign on Teague's Antiques, the dogwoods planted on the town hall lawn, the color of the window shutters along Lawyers Row.

"Are you lost?"

I turned around. "Excuse me?"

Two guys were sprawled on a bench close to the sidewalk. The one who had spoken wore tattered shorts and a colonial three-cornered hat—nothing else. He had wide shoulders and long, muscular legs. He stretched dramatically, then lay his tanned arms along the back of the bench. "You look lost," he said. "Can I help you find something?"

"Uh, no, thanks. I was just looking."

He grinned. "Me, too."

"Oh?" I glanced around, thinking I'd missed something. "At what?"

He and his friend burst out laughing.

Way to go, Lauren, I thought. He had been looking at *me!* He was flirting.

Feeling stupid, I stuck my hands in my pockets and kept walking. I knew I was blushing.

"Have a good time looking," he called after me.

I turned halfway around. "Thanks."

On the one-to-ten scale of the girls at Birch Hill, he was a definite *eight,* maybe higher if he took off the hat. I could see from the slight tilt of his head that he was assigning a number to me, too. I turned back quickly and kept walking.

"Make sure you stop at the dunking booth," he added. "It's part of the festival, two blocks down. See you in about ten minutes."

I glanced over my shoulder. "Okay . . . maybe." I felt the warmth spreading on the back of my neck and wondered if the backs of my legs were pink as well.

Would he really meet me there? But then what? Nothing, of course. I was good at math and English, and good at sports, but lousy at guys. Of course, a girls' boarding school didn't allow for much experience with guys, but the real reason was that when I got the chance, I ducked it.

I wondered if Aunt Jule's daughters were dating a lot now. My godmother visited me twice a year and downloaded me on everything I had done, but she always brushed off my questions about Nora and Holly with short answers. And she never remembered to bring photos, so I couldn't even picture them as teens. Maybe Nora and Holly knew this guy, I thought, then put him out of my mind.

The two and a half blocks from Washington Street to the town harbor were closed off to cars for the festival. I began to wander through the tents set up in the street. At a political booth I said a silent hello to my father. An unflattering picture of his face was blown up to beach-ball size and nicely framed by a red circle, a diagonal line drawn through it—the banning symbol. The farmers and watermen on the Eastern Shore hated his political agenda; if I were them, I would, too.

I passed the Mallard, a colonial tavern converted to a bed-and-breakfast, then stopped in at Tea Leaves Café, where the best cookies in the world were made. Standing inside the door, I enjoyed the cool draft from the ceiling fans and the rich, familiar smells of brown sugar and butter. Then a feeling of dread spread through me. My skin prickled with sweat and turned ice cold. I remembered sitting in the café as a little girl, watching my mother slowly descend the steps from the second floor, where fortunes were told.

Mommy's face was the color of pale icing. Old Miss Lydia had peered into her crystal ball and seen grave danger and death. When my mother told me that—like a fact, not a prediction—I was so scared I cried. I didn't know how I could protect her.

Looking back on it now, I realized that Miss Lydia hadn't needed a crystal ball to make such a dark prediction. After a hundred tabloid stories about my father's romances and my mother's wealth, and having endured years of cruel comments from political advisers who saw my mother as a liability, she had come to believe that everyone was against her—everyone except me. She had clung to me as if I were a life preserver. Fear and anger had been written on her face, and that was all the fortune-teller needed to read.

I left the café and continued on, barely seeing the

shops and booths I passed. Not until I crossed Cannon Street did I come back to the present, startled back into it by an amplified voice.

"Come on, all you spaghetti arms! Who's going to wind up and throw that ball? You there—come on, skinny. Put me out of my misery. Dunk me!"

It was the guy from the bench, still wearing his three-cornered hat. He razzed the fairgoers from a plank suspended above a vat of water. According to the sign, the dunking booth was raising money for Wisteria High School.

Two middle-aged men took the bait and threw at the target, a four-inch disk which, if struck, would upend the plank.

"Nice curve ball, buddy. Too bad it was five feet off. Come on, girls, your turn. Show that guy how it's done."

Several groups of girls about my age had gathered around the booth, and guys were hanging out to watch the girls hanging out. There was a lot of body language going on—a glance over a bare shoulder, the sweep of eyelashes, the lifting of long waves of hair. I could learn something from these girls, I thought—not that I planned to use it anytime soon.

"Come on, limber up those pretty arms," the guy with the hat urged. "Want me to make the target bigger? How big? Big as a beach towel? Think you could hit that?"

I could, I thought. I could peg that little red disk. But I stayed at the back of the crowd, observing the flirting.

"Hey, it's the looker!" he announced with delight. "I

didn't think you'd show, looker. Step right up! Why're you standing all the way back there?"

I glanced to the left and the right, hoping someone would materialize next to me.

"*You,*" he said.

Everyone in the crowd turned to me. I've been stared at in Washington, where people know I'm "Brandt's daughter," and I've learned to shut it out. But this was different. My instincts told me I couldn't shut *him* out.

"You're not shy, are you?"

"Shy of what?"

Some of the kids laughed. I hadn't meant to be funny.

"Shy of showing off that arm."

"No," I said.

He waited for me to say more. There was a long pause. I felt as if I were back in the days when my father would call me up to the speaker's podium and I was supposed to say something cute. I remained stubbornly silent.

"Then come on up. Do everybody a favor and shut me up," he said. "Put down your money, pick up that ball, and let it fly, looker."

"I'd rather not."

People laughed.

He flapped his arms and squawked like a chicken. "Afraid you can't throw that far?"

"I know I can."

He lifted his hat in a small salute to my claim. Blond curls slipped out, then he plopped the hat back on and said, "I dare you."

The guy with whom he had been sitting on the bench put down a dollar and motioned to me.

"Come on," the blond guy taunted from the dunking bench. "Show us some muscle."

This is what you find in a small town, I thought, guys from the last century when it comes to their attitude toward girls.

I made my way to the front of the crowd. The guy on the plank started singing what must have been the Wisteria High School anthem. His buddy handed me a softball. I focused on the target, imagining it was the first baseman's glove at Birch Hill and we needed one more out to win the championship. I planted my feet and threw.

Bull's-eye! He went down on a high note.

The crowd cheered loudly. For a moment all we saw was the floating hat, then his blond head popped up.

"Lucky shot," he said.

"No way," I replied.

"Law of chance. Eventually someone had to hit the target."

"Want to try for two?" I asked.

"Twice lucky? I don't think so."

I grabbed a ball and raised my arm, ready to nail the target.

"Hey—hey! Wait till I get back on the bench." He reclaimed his hat and climbed up onto the plank. "And somebody's got to pay."

I pulled a dollar from my shorts.

"Okay, girls and guys, let's see if this looker is—" He swallowed the rest.

There were more cheers and shouts of "Do it again! Do it again!"

People started laying down money. I had never been surrounded by so many cute guys. I lost my nerve and backed away from the booth. "Sorry, I, uh, have to go."

"Three in a row, three in a row!" someone shouted. Others picked up the chant.

"No, really, I have to go."

Out of the corner of my eye I saw a woman with camera equipment turn in our direction. I can pick out a press ID tag a mile away.

"Please let me through," I begged, but the crowd pushed forward. I glanced over at the guy standing waist deep in the water and expected him to start taunting me again.

He met my eyes, then reached for his megaphone. "I'm not getting back on that bench," he said, "not till little Miss Lucky leaves."

"Aw, come on," the crowd urged.

"No way." He set down the megaphone, then flopped on his back. With his hat resting on his stomach, he floated and sang "God Bless America."

Two guys began to goad him. I slipped behind them, dodged three more, and made my escape, not stopping until I reached Water Street. There I leaned against a tree and silently thanked the tease for letting me off the hook.

A short block ahead of me was the glittering Sycamore River. I gazed at it for several minutes, remembering long, lazy afternoons of watching it from Aunt Jule's porch, back when it sparkled with nothing but happy memories. A wet hand suddenly touched my shoulder.

"Remember me?"

I turned quickly and found the blond guy grinning at me, dripping on the ground around him, the corners of his hat sagging. I tried to think of something clever to say; unable to, I said nothing.

"Are you shy?" he asked.

"No, not at all, not around people I know."

He laughed. "That's brave of you. What's your name?"

"Lauren."

"Want to go out, Lauren?"

I blinked. "Jeez! No."

He blinked back at me, as surprised by my answer as I was by his question.

I fumbled for an excuse. "I'm not going to be here very long," I lied.

"Perfect!" he replied. "My dating policy is one date per girl. Occasionally, I go on two dates with the same girl, but that's my absolute limit. I don't want to get hooked. You like movies?"

"But I don't even know you," I argued.

"You want references? I have college recommendations. They don't talk about my excellent ability with girls, but—"

I glanced quickly to the right. A girl was watching us, most of her hidden by an artist's easel and the flap of a tent. All I could see were her dark eyes, eyes that were drawn together, as if in pain or anger. When she realized I saw her, she turned and disappeared.

"Hey," the guy said, touching me on the elbow, studying my face, "don't take me so seriously."

I glanced back at him.

"It's no big deal," he went on. "I can stand rejection. I'll just be crushed for months."

I smiled a little. "Maybe you know Nora and Holly—"

"Ingram?" he finished quickly.

"Their mother is my godmother."

His eyes widened. He took a step closer, peering down at me. I was very aware of the the strong line of his jaw and the curve of his mouth.

Ten, I thought, *he's definitely a* ten.

"You're Lauren Brandt," he said. "I should have known it. You still have those chocolate-kiss eyes."

I took a step back.

"Here." He plunked his wet hat on my head. "Don't go anywhere," he told me, then turned away. When he faced me again, his eyes were crossed and his mouth stretched wide by his fingers. "Now do you recognize me?"

"Nick? Nick Hurley?" I asked, laughing.

He took back his hat. "You'll be sorry to hear I don't make gross faces as much as I used to. Now I'd rather smile at girls."

"I noticed."

He waved his hat around as if trying to dry it, his green eyes sparkling at me, as full of fun and trouble as when he was in elementary school. I relaxed. This was my old buddy. We used to fish and crab together and have slimy bait battles with chopped-up eels and raw chicken parts.

"You've changed," he said. "You're—uh—"

"Yes?"

"Taller."

"I hope so. I was ten the last time you saw me."

"And your hair's really dark now—and short," he added.

My mother had loved long hair and fussed with mine constantly. The year after she died, I cut if off and haven't grown it since.

"Other things have changed, too," he said, his eyes laughing again. "Where are you staying?"

"At Aunt Jule's," I replied. "Does your uncle Frank still live next to her?"

"Yup, and he and Jule still don't get along, my parents still live on the other side of Oyster Creek, and Mom still teaches at the college. Things haven't changed much around here." His face grew more serious. "You know, I waited for you to come back the summer after your mother died. And the one after that. When the third summer came and you didn't, I figured you never would."

I shrugged, as if things had just turned out that way.

"So why did you finally return?" he asked bluntly.

I told him the least personal reason. "Aunt Jule said she had to see me and insisted that it be in Wisteria."

His face broke into a sunny smile. "I'm glad she did. Listen, I have to get back. Tim is covering for me at the dunking booth."

I nodded.

"See you around, " he said.

"Yeah, see you," I replied, and continued to watch

him as he walked away. He turned around suddenly and caught me staring, then he grinned in a self-assured way that told me he was used to girls admiring him. I could never have predicted that the round-cheeked boy whose feet were always caked with river mud would turn out like this.

I glanced at my watch. Aunt Jule would be expecting me—not that she had ever stuck to a schedule, but she knew I did. I retraced my steps, pausing for a moment at a table of handmade jewelry.

Her again—the girl I had seen before. This time she was hiding in the narrow space between two brick houses, watching me from the shadows.

Was she a friend of Nick's? I wondered, feeling uncomfortable. Perhaps she was someone who had dated him once and never gotten over him. Why else would she be watching me?

You're acting the way Mom used to, I chided myself; someone looks at you twice and you read into it. It's just a coincidence.

Wanting to avoid another scene at the dunking booth, I took a detour onto Shipwrights Street and stopped to admire an herb garden in a tiny front yard. There she was again! I found it disturbing that someone with such unhappy eyes would shadow me. At the end of the block I returned to High Street, feeling safer in a crowd.

I had parked my Honda in front of the old newsstand and stopped there to pick up a local paper. As I stood at the counter inside, I remembered buying a pile of magazines and comic books after my mother's funeral. My father, hoping to comfort me, had given me a twenty to spend and waited in the car, talking to his advisers by phone. I remembered looking at the tabloids that day, reading their glaring headlines: SENATOR'S WIFE MURDERED, SENATOR STOPS INVESTIGATION.

But it wasn't my father who kept the police at bay the night my mother died and in the weeks following. Aunt Jule had argued fiercely with the sheriff and the state police, insisting the drowning was an accident, begging them for my sake not to stir up rumors with a pointless investigation.

Aunt Jule, whose long roots in this town gave her more clout than my father, had been my protector, and the house where my mother felt haunted, my refuge. The headlines made me cringe, but I had been taught that tabloids lied. And I never stopped to wonder if my mother's death was truly an accident or if Aunt Jule might have been protecting someone other than me.

three

I bounced my way over the potholes of Aunt Jule's driveway, past her rusty Volvo, and thumped to a stop. From the driver's seat I gazed up at the house, hoping it would look as I remembered. In most ways it did.

The long rectangular frame of the house was covered with gray clapboard. Its double set of porches, upper and lower, ran from end to end and a wood stairway led down from the upper porch. Along both porches there were doors rather than windows, each room having at least one exit to the outside. But unlike the pristine image I carried in my mind, the doors sagged with potbellied screens, and the paint was peeling badly. The river side of the house, which was identical to the garden side but exposed to the water, probably looked worse.

I climbed out of the car. The pungent smell of boxwood and the fragrance of roses surrounded me—just as

I remembered! Between the house and myself were two big gardens, a square knot garden on the right, bristling with bushy hedges and herbs, and a flower garden on the left.

"Lauren! You're here!" Aunt Jule cried out happily, stepping onto the lower porch. "Do you need help with your suitcase? Holly," she called.

No matter what clothes Aunt Jule bought, she always seemed to be wearing the same outfit—a denim skirt or pants with a loose print top. Her long brown hair had streaks of gray in it now and fell in a thick braid down her back.

We met at the head of the path between the knot and flower gardens.

She threw her arms around me. "Hello, love. It's good to have you back."

"It's good to be back," I said, hugging her tightly.

"I've missed you."

"And I've missed you." I saw Holly emerging from the house. "But promise you won't make a fuss over me."

When I was a little girl, my godmother would welcome me like visiting royalty and wait on me for the first few days. Holly would get so mad she wouldn't speak to me. It was only when Nora and Nick did, and she felt left out, that she would warm up and assume her usual position of ringleader.

Holly strode toward us, taller now than both her mother and I. Her shoulder-length hair was almost black, a glorious, shimmering color that contrasted sharply with her blue eyes. She had the beautiful eyes and brows of an actress, the kind that caught your attention with their drama and careful shaping.

"You look great!" I said.

She hugged me. "You, too. Welcome back, Lauren. I was so excited when Mom said you were coming. Is there something I can carry?"

I opened the trunk of my car, took out a full-size suitcase, and handed her an overnight bag.

Aunt Jule hovered close by and touched the smaller bag's soft leather. "How nice!" she said. "You should get one of these, Holly."

"Right, Mom. Shall we put it on our credit card? Come inside, Lauren. You must be thirsty," Holly said, starting up the path.

"Oh, Lord!" Aunt Jule's hand flew up to her forehead. "I forgot to check what we have to drink. There could be—"

"Iced tea or lemonade," Holly told me, smiling. "I made a pitcher of each. Which would you like?"

"Iced tea, please."

My godmother and I followed Holly into the house, entering the back of a wide hall that ran from the garden side to the river side of the house. We set my bags at the foot of the stairs and turned right, into the dining room.

It looked exactly as I remembered—a collection of dark wood chairs scattered around a long table that was buried beneath mail, magazines, and baskets of Aunt Jule's craft stuff. The mahogany table might have been a valuable antique, but it was badly scarred by years of water rings and the grind of game pieces into its surface. One reason I had loved to come here was that, unlike my parents' elegant town house, it was almost impossible to "ruin" something.

In the kitchen Holly set four glasses on a tray and began to pour the tea.

"Where's Nora?" I asked.

"She'll come around sooner or later," Aunt Jule replied casually.

Holly glanced sharply at her mother. "I assume you told Lauren about Nora."

"Not yet. Lauren has just arrived."

"You should have told her before."

"I saw no point in saying anything until she came," Aunt Jule replied coolly, then smiled at me. "Garden room or river room?"

"Garden."

Holly picked up the tray. "Don't forget to turn out the light, Mom."

"Forget? How can I, with you always reminding me?"

"I don't know, but somehow you do."

As we left the kitchen I peeked at Holly, wondering what I was supposed to be told about Nora. She had not been the most normal of kids.

We passed through the hall again and entered the garden room. Aunt Jule's house was built in the early 1900s on the foundation of a much older one that had burned down. Intended as a summer home, it was designed for airiness. The dining room and kitchen lay on one side of the stairs and, together with the steps and hall, occupied a third of the space downstairs. On the other side of the hall were two long rectangular rooms, each with two sets of double porch doors, those in one room facing the garden, those in the other facing the river. Two wide doorways connected these rooms, allowing the breeze to blow through the house.

At Aunt Jule's you never felt far from the Sycamore River. Each time I took a breath I noticed the mustiness that shore homes seem to have in their bones. And I knew I still wasn't ready to face the dock where my mother had struck her head, or the water below it, where she had drowned.

We had just settled down in the garden room with its two lumpy sofas and assortment of stuffed chairs when Nora entered from the porch. I was startled at what I saw.

"Nora, dear, Lauren has arrived," Aunt Jule said.

Nora stood silently and stared at me. Her thin, black hair was pulled straight back in an old plastic headband and hung in short, oily pieces. Her dark eyes were troubled. The slight frown she wore as a child had deepened into a single, vertical crease between her eyebrows, a line of anger or worry that couldn't be erased.

"Please say hello, Nora," Aunt Jule coaxed softly.

Nora acted as if she hadn't heard. She crossed the room to a table on which sat a vase of roses. She began to rearrange the flowers, her mouth set in a grim line.

"Hi, Nora. It's good to see you," I said.

She pricked her finger on a thorn and pulled her hand away quickly.

"It's good to see you again," I told her.

This time she met my eyes. Locking her gaze on

mine, she reached for the rose stem and pricked her finger deliberately, repeatedly.

Her strange behavior did not seem to faze anyone else. Holly leaned forward in her chair, blocking my view of Nora. "So, did my mother think to tell you I'm graduating?"

"Uh, yes," I replied, turning my attention to her. "It's this coming Thursday, right? She said this was Senior Week for you. Are kids getting all weepy about saying goodbye?"

Holly grimaced. "Not me. I'm editor in chief of our yearbook. And the prom's tomorrow, my swim party Tuesday night. I'm too busy to get sentimental."

"I can help you get ready for the party," I offered. "Cleaning, fixing food, whatever. It'll be fun."

"I wish you hadn't come," Nora said.

I sat back in my seat, surprised, and turned to look at her.

She said nothing more, continuing to arrange the flowers with intense concentration.

"Ignore her," said Holly.

"She'll get used to you," Aunt Jule added.

Used to me? I grew up with Nora.

"We had some hot days in May," Holly went on, "so the water's plenty warm for an evening swim party."

"Don't go near the water," warned Nora.

"The whole class is coming," Holly went on, as if her sister hadn't spoken.

I heard Nora leave the room.

"I'm borrowing amplifiers from Frank—and torches and strings of light," Holly added.

"I told you not to," Aunt Jule remarked.

"And I ignored you," Holly said, then turned to me. "You remember Frank, from next door?"

I nodded. "Yes, I saw his neph—"

I broke off at the sound of a crash in the next room. Aunt Jule and Holly glanced at each other, then the three of us rushed into the river room.

Nora was standing five feet from an end table, gazing down at a broken ceramic lamp. She seemed fascinated by it. I heard Aunt Jule take a deep breath and let it out again.

"Nora!" Holly exclaimed. "That was a good lamp."

"I didn't do it," Nora replied quickly.

"You should watch where you're going," Holly persisted.

"But I didn't do it." Nora glanced around the room. "Someone else did."

I bent down to pick up the pieces of the shattered base. The lamp's cord had been pulled from the wall socket and was tied in a knot. When I saw it, the skin on my neck prickled. I thought about the things my mother had found knotted in her room just before she died.

A coincidence, I told myself, then untied the cord.

When I looked up, Nora was watching me, her dark eyes gleaming as if she had just solved a puzzled. "You did it," she said.

"Of course I didn't."

"Then *she* did."

"She?" I asked. "Who?"

"Now that you're here, there's no stopping her," Nora whispered.

"I don't understand."

Holly dismissed our puzzling conversation with a wave of her hand. "Leave that, Lauren," she said. "Nora broke it and Nora will clean it up. Come on, let's take your things upstairs. I'll help you unpack."

I glanced uncertainly at Aunt Jule, but she smiled as if everything were fine. "That would be lovely of you, Holly. I'll handle things down here."

Holly and I picked up my baggage in the hall and climbed the steps, which rose to the garden side of the house, then turned in the direction of the river side. Arriving in the upper hall, I felt as if I were ten again, breathing in the sweet cedar scent of the closets and the smell of the river.

A door to the upper porch was straight ahead. Aunt Jule's room was to the right, her bedroom facing the water, her private sitting room facing the garden. The hall to the left of the stairs led to four bedrooms.

"You're in the same room as always. Is that okay?" Holly asked.

"Sure," I replied, not so sure.

We passed Holly's room to the right, facing the water, and Nora's, which was directly across from her sister's, looking out on the garden. The next door to the right was mine.

I entered the bedroom and turned away from the door-length view of the river, focusing on the furniture. The oak chest, dresser, and plain oak bed with a blue-and-white quilt looked just as I had left them. The varnished wood floor had the same braid rug coiled in a circle. A small fireplace, which had been walled up as long as I could remember, still had a collection of old paperbacks on its narrow shelf. We set my suitcases on the bed.

"Thanks, Holly. Thanks for making me welcome, fixing the tea and all."

"Are you kidding? I'm glad you're here," she replied, sitting on a straight-back chair, then quickly standing up again. Its cane seat was worn through. "I'm just sorry the house is such a disaster. You know my mother. Not exactly the queen of mommies and housewives."

I laughed. "That's why I loved it here. It always felt so free and easy. But I guess her way of living is not as much fun now, not if you're the one who has to handle everything."

Holly tilted her head to one side, as if surprised. "I didn't think you'd understand that. Not *you.*"

She had always said I was spoiled. My parents had certainly given me enough to be, and it didn't help when Aunt Jule would treat me like a little princess. My last visit to Wisteria had been particularly hard on Holly and Nora, with both Aunt Jule and my mother fussing and fighting over me. Worse, my mother, who could be quite snobby about the children with whom I played, had constantly criticized Nora and Holly.

"I guess you know money is tight around here," Holly said. "Mom should sell the place, but she won't. Frank's been making good offers. He's been doing a lot of real estate development, and, of course, he'd love to have property next to his own, but she won't speak to him. Meanwhile we have old bills to pay—gas and electric, phone, taxes. Our credit cards are maxed." She shook her head. "Sorry, I didn't mean to dump on you. Let's get you unpacked."

I opened my suitcase. "I can help you out with the bills."

"Oh, no!" she protested.

"Holly, you know my father—he gives checks, not hugs. I have a large bank account from him, and when I'm eighteen, I inherit all of my mother's estate. I didn't earn any of the money. It's just there—there to be used. How much do you need?"

I could see her trying to decide what to say. "Do you have access to the family account?" I asked. "Do you have a checkbook?"

She nodded slowly. "I'm the one who writes the checks now, when there's money."

"So figure out what you need and let me know. I'll transfer the funds tomorrow when the bank opens. Really, it makes sense," I argued. "You want to keep your credit good."

"My mother would kill me if she knew I—"

"So don't tell her," I said. "She probably doesn't even look at your bank statements."

Holly burst out laughing. "You've got that right." She plopped down on the bed and stretched back against the pillow. It seemed easier to be with her now that we were older.

"Holly, what's going on with Nora?"

She turned on her side and picked through my open bag the way she used to go through my Barbie carry-case. "I'm really worried," she said at last. "I'm sure you can tell she's gotten worse. I guess Mom told you she didn't finish high school."

I shook my head no. "Your mother can be very silent about some things."

"Nora barely made it to her sixteenth birthday. I think the teachers passed her each year because they wanted to get rid of her."

"But she's not dumb," I said.

"No," Holly replied, "just crazy. Do you remember when you were here how she had started to fear water?"

"Yeah. The last summer I came, she would go out on the dock, but was afraid to dangle her feet over it, afraid to be splashed."

"Well, she's totally phobic now—about water, about all kinds of things. She never leaves the property."

I frowned. "Not at all?"

"No. She needs a psychiatrist—badly—but Mom won't do anything about it. It seems like Nora is getting weirder every day. It's scary." Holly sat up. "I mean, I'm sure she's not dangerous. She wouldn't hurt anyone. But she doesn't reason like a normal person. She gets angry when there's nothing to be angry at, and she imagines people are after her."

Like my mother, I thought. It was as if something in this house—I banished the idea, reminding myself that my mother's problems started before we came to Wisteria.

"She's always had an active imagination," I recalled.

Holly let out a sharp laugh. "You sound like my mother. *Nora's just imaginative. Nora's just sensitive. Nora's just going through adolescence.* Remember how'd she say that the summer your mother was here?"

I nodded, recalling Nora's sudden outbursts of anger and tears and Aunt Jule's quiet explanations. I used to hear Nora on the porch outside my bedroom, talking to herself, answering questions that no one asked.

"Well," said Holly, "it's been a very long adolescence."

I tugged opened a drawer and dropped in my T-shirts. "You said she's totally phobic. Is there anyone she trusts—anyone she can talk to?"

"Myself, Mom, and Nick. Remember Nick Hurley, Frank's nephew?"

"Yes. I—"

"You might want to steer clear of Nora except when I'm around," Holly suggested, rising, then walking to the hall door. "I know her better than anyone, and it's hard even for me to guess what will set her off."

I saw the shadow on the hallway wall, cast by someone leaning forward to hear our words.

"Just till she gets used to you being here, of course."

The shadow pulled back, as if sensing that Holly was about to leave.

"Do you remember where the towels are? Is there anything else I can get you?" Holly asked.

"I'm fine, thanks."

She left me to finish unpacking and to puzzle over the situation I had walked into. Maybe Holly did know Nora better than anyone, but she didn't know everything. Nora left the property sometimes; it was she who had shadowed me at the festival.

four

Seven years ago I awakened from what I thought was a horrible nightmare. I rushed to my mother's room, wanting her to tell me it hadn't happened, but she wasn't there. I ran to Aunt Jule's. She, too, was gone.

I raced downstairs, out of the house, and down to the water. It was barely dawn, with just a hint of pink in the pearl gray sky. Aunt Jule was standing at the end of the dock, staring at a piling, one of the weathered posts that supported the long walkway. When she heard my footsteps on the wooden planks, she spun around.

In her hands were a bucket and scrub brush. As I got closer to her, I smelled bleach. Aunt Jule opened her mouth as if to tell me to go back, but it was too late. I saw that the piling was stained—dark-colored, reddish. It was blood, my mother's blood. I threw up.

I haven't been back to the dock since that morning, though I'd spent three more weeks at Aunt Jule's, until my father could arrange for a baby-sitter in Washington. Now I needed to see the place where my mother had fallen, to walk out on the dock and touch the piling that had been scoured clean by Aunt Jule and years of rain. Still, the thought of it made my stomach cramp.

I stood on the porch outside my bedroom, gazing at the peaceful river, looking well past the dock, farther out to the misty line between bay and sky. It was that view that Aunt Jule loved and that made her property so valuable.

The Chesapeake Bay washes northward through the widest part of Maryland, and the Sycamore River branches off the bay in a northeasterly direction. Surrounded on three sides by water—the Sycamore and two big creeks—the town of Wisteria sits on a piece of land that appears to jut into the river. Because the town is close to the wide river mouth, you can see the bay from one side of it. Aunt Jule's house is on that side at the very end of Bayview Avenue, built on land that extends beyond the corner of Bayview and Water Street.

According to my mother, the Ingram family once had a ton of money. They had owned several houses and sent their children to exclusive schools like Birch Hill, which is where my mother and godmother became friends. But generation after generation had mismanaged the wealth. Now all Aunt Jule had was the house and the land, which is all she wanted, if you ask me. She had been married briefly to Holly and Nora's father, but he had wanted to see the world and she didn't want to leave her home. Several years after he left Wisteria, he died.

I had no idea how she paid her bills. Abandoned craft projects were strewn through the house. She was very talented, but didn't have the discipline to earn a living that way. Still, I had never seen her worry about money. Somehow, whatever she needed materialized.

I reentered the house and headed downstairs. When I reached the bottom of the steps, I heard voices in the dining room.

"It's just common sense, Mother," Holly said. "You know you've never been able to handle a camera. Remember the pictures you took before the Christmas dance? None of us had feet."

"I don't find feet all that interesting," Aunt Jule replied.

"They are when Jackie and I each spend big bucks on shoes," Holly countered. "I told you that at the time." Seeing me at the doorway, she gave a little wave. Aunt Jule glanced up from her quilting.

"Anyway, like it or not," Holly continued, "Frank's coming over and taking pictures before the prom. Nick's parents are going to want photos, too, and—"

"Nick?" I repeated, entering the room.

"Nick Hurley," she replied, smiling.

"Mr. Frank's nephew?"

"Yes. We're dating."

I looked at her, surprised. *Two's the limit*, I almost said, but maybe that was just a line he had given me.

"We've been friends forever, of course," she went on. "Now Nick has finally seen the light. And if he hasn't, he will," she added, laughing.

I laughed with her and squelched my disappointment.

"Wait till you see him," Holly said. "He's not that round-faced kid anymore."

"I know. I ran into him at the festival on my way here. I dunked him twice at your school booth."

"You were at the festival?" The smile disappeared from Holly's face. "At my school's dunking booth?"

"I was walking through town and happened to pass it," I replied. I didn't tell her that Nick had asked me to stop by, for I had just gotten the same chilly feeling I used to get around Holly, as if I were invading her territory.

But then she smiled. "He's coming around later. It'll be like old times."

"I guess you visited Sondra's grave," Aunt Jule said to me.

"I didn't, but I will tomorrow. I need to do things one at a time," I explained. "It—it's kind of hard coming back here. For me Wisteria is not all happy memories."

"We're well beyond those unhappy times," Aunt Jule observed. "Seven years beyond."

"Still, when I came back today, it seemed like yesterday."

"That's why you shouldn't have waited so long," she replied.

Her cool tone surprised me. "My mother died here," I said defensively. "You can't expect me to think of it as a great vacation spot."

"It's where you were born," Aunt Jule answered firmly. "It's where you had your happiest times."

"Yes, but—"

"It's time you got over Sondra's death, Lauren. She wasn't exactly Mother of the Year."

That stung. "I know, but she was my mother. Excuse me, I'm going for a walk."

I turned abruptly and exited through the dining room door to the porch. I had thought Aunt Jule would be more understanding, but a trace of that summer's bitterness had remained with her. It seemed to me that Aunt Jule, herself, hadn't completely left that time behind.

I took the three steps down to the grass, paused to look at the dock, then walked the long slope down to it. The river's edge was a spongy mix of mud, sand, and clay, tufted with long bay grass. Aunt Jule's property was probably the only shoreline in Wisteria unprotected by a sea wall. The dock no longer met the riverbank, the land having eroded from beneath it.

Planting my hands on the dock, I swung my feet up onto it, as if climbing onto a three-foot wall. I stood up slowly, my eyes traveling the length of the T-shaped walkway, then shifting to the far left side, to the piling where my mother had struck her head.

She may have been drinking. It was easy to trip on the uneven planks. The tide was high that night, the water just over her head. It took so little for a person to die. Aunt Jule had told me over and over that it was nobody's fault.

And yet, I felt responsible. My mother had refused to let me visit Aunt Jule that last summer. But the more clingy she had become, the more desperate I'd been to get away from her. I had thrown fierce tantrums until she gave in—gave in with the condition that she would accompany me. If I hadn't argued, if we hadn't come, would she still be alive?

I couldn't walk to the end of the dock, not yet. I jumped down and climbed the hill to the house.

My mother had become even worse in Wisteria, still clinging, not wanting me to play with Nora and Holly. She would blame them for things. She'd tell me I was too good for them, and say it in front of them. Poor Holly had been caught between snubbing me entirely and acting like my best and dearest friend—just to get my mother riled.

Both Holly and Nora had fought back with words, showing the anger that I myself felt but tried to hide. Then Mommy drowned. What do you do with your anger when the person you're mad at goes off and dies? Bury it? Bury it inside you?

I circled the house to see the gardens, hoping they could still give me the peace I had felt there as a child. I passed my favorite tree, a huge old oak with a swing. Someone had lassoed the high branch with a new rope. The gardens, too, had been cared for and looked better than they had seven years ago. My heart lightened.

A greenhouse stood not far from the garden, a long rectangular structure with a gambrel roof, built in the 1930s on the brick base of an earlier one. The roof vents were up and the door open.

When I peeked in I found Nora tending plants halfway down the main aisle, on one of the short cross aisles. Focused on her work, her fingers moving deftly among the shiny leaves, she didn't notice me. I stepped inside the door and she looked up. Her eyes darted fearfully around the greenhouse. I thought that she had heard me enter, but her gaze passed over me as if I were invisible. I, too, looked around, wondering what she sensed.

She started to tremble and shook her head with quick, jerky motions. It was as if she had something frightening inside it that she was trying to shake out. I remembered as a child how she hated getting water in her ears and would become frantic to get rid of it. I watched silently, afraid to speak and upset her more.

The shaking finally stopped, the fear in her easing into a quiet wariness. She tended her plants, neatly removing yellow leaves. I surveyed the greenhouse again. There was nothing there—nothing that I could see—triggering her emotions; whatever Nora was reacting to was deep inside her.

"Hi, Nora."

This time when she looked up, she saw me. "I don't want you here."

I walked toward her. "Here in the greenhouse or here at your mother's?"

She didn't answer.

"Why don't you want me around?" I asked.

She moved on to another bench of plants and began to snip off their tops.

"Nora, why don't you like me anymore?"

"I don't remember."

"Please try to."

She pressed her lips together and nervously fingered dark strings of hair. I wished Aunt Jule would make her wash it.

"I'm busy," she said. "I have to cut off their little heads. It hurts them. They hate it, but they will be better for it."

"You mean you're pinching back the plants so they'll grow bushier?" I asked.

"Do you want to see my vines?" she replied.

I wasn't sure if she was too mentally scattered to answer my questions or simply unwilling. "Sure."

She led me outside and showed me several trellises standing against the southern wall.

"It gets too hot in the summer, so I use the climbers to shade the plants inside. These are morning glories," she said, pointing to the heart-shaped leaves. "And over there is Lauren."

"Laurel?" I asked, misunderstanding her. "It looks like a climbing rose."

"It is. I named her Lauren."

"Oh." I wondered if it was a coincidence that she had given the plant my name. "Then we're called the same thing," I remarked cheerfully.

But Nora was frowning now, the vertical crease between her eyes deepening, the troubled world inside her more real to her than the one outside.

"Will you get me some fishing line?" she asked. "I use it to tie up Lauren. Morning glories will twine themselves. But roses have to be tied or else their arms will fall and strike you, and their thorns will make you bleed."

I mulled over her strange way of describing her work, trying to understand what lay behind the words.

"There's fishing line in the boathouse. Will you get it?" she asked. "I don't go in there. It's full of water."

"No problem," I said.

"You'll need the key."

"It's locked? Why?" I asked.

Nora twisted her hands. "Because she's in there. She goes there to sleep during the day."

"Who?"

"Sondra."

My breath caught in my throat. "You mean my mother? She's dead."

"She sleeps there during the day," Nora replied. "Be quiet when you go in or you will wake her."

She was serious. A chill went up my spine.

"I'll show you where the key is," Nora said, walking backward a few steps, then turning to hurry on.

About thirty feet from the boathouse she stopped. Standing next to her, I surveyed the old building, which was nestled in the bank where the river curved, straddling the border between Aunt Jule's and Mr. Frank's property. The boathouse had deteriorated badly. Its roof buckled, two shutters hung off their hinges, and many of the wood shingles were broken. As far back as I could remember, there hadn't been a boat in the house. We used to put our crab traps there and fish off its roof. Now we'd probably fall through.

"Do you see her?" Nora whispered.

"No."

"She's asleep," Nora said, her voice barely audible. "All night she swims out by the dock, then she comes here at dawn. She wants to stay in the darkness."

"That makes no sense," I replied in a voice too loud. "Why would she do that?"

"She's looking for her little girl."

My throat felt tight when I swallowed. I strode ahead and found both the land entrance and the doors to the river closed and padlocked. The shutters were loose, but the windows were boarded up.

"Where's the key?" I asked.

"On a hook behind the shutter," Nora said, hanging back.

I found the key and unlocked the padlock. Nora crept closer. I laid the padlock on the ground, pulled back the latch, then opened the door.

After being in the bright sunlight, I couldn't see a thing. Cautiously I stepped inside. The smell of stagnant water, earth, and rot was overwhelming. It wouldn't be hard to believe that someone was dead in here.

I remembered there was a narrow walkway lining three sides of the building, surrounding the area of water where a boat would float. Along the wall to the right there used to be a light with a pull-chain. I felt my way toward it.

"Where's the line kept, Nora?" I called out to her.

"In the loft," she answered softly.

Great. I'd probably climb into a rat colony. But I went on, hoping that in helping Nora I'd win her trust, as well as prove to her that my mother wasn't here. I felt the beaded chain and yanked down hard. Nothing. I reached up and touched an empty socket.

At least my eyes were adjusting. I saw the outline of

the ladder to the loft just a few feet ahead of me and started toward it.

"Don't close the door, Nora," I called to her. "I need all the light I can get. Did you hear? I said don't—"

The door shut.

"Nora? Nora!" I shouted. "No-ra!"

five

It was pitch black inside. I kept my hands on the wall and took a step toward the door. "All right, Nora," I called, struggling to keep my voice calm, "what are you doing?"

Metal scraped against metal. She was fastening the padlock.

"Nora!"

I rushed toward the door. My toe caught on the uneven boards and I pitched headlong in the dark. My fingers touched the ledge of a window frame but slipped off. I teetered on the edge of the walkway, my ankle wobbling. I couldn't stand the thought of falling into the foul water, the water where Nora said my mother slept.

I caught my balance again and sank down on my knees. I didn't care whether Nora was playing a prank or truly afraid, I was angry. I banged my fists against the wall. "Nora! Let me out!"

Her voice was faint. "Lauren?"

"This isn't funny," I said. "Unlock the door."

"She's awake!" Nora cried out.

"What?"

"She's awake!" Nora sounded out of breath, as if she were running away.

"Come back here."

There was no reply. I rested my head against the wall, thinking about what to do. Then, in the oppressive darkness and silence, I heard it: the movement of water, its restless shift from side to side in the boathouse. I couldn't see the water, but I could hear it, slapping the walls, tumbling back on itself. Something was stirring it up.

I listened as it grew more turbulent. Was it some animal? Had one gotten through the tangle of nets abandoned at the entrance? Something was in the water, something Nora must have heard or seen before.

She's looking for her little girl, Nora had said. I shivered. My mother was always looking for me, panicking as soon as I'd disappear from sight. I cowered against the boathouse wall and flinched with each slap of the water, feeling—or imagining—water droplets on my arms.

Then the lapping grew softer. The water became eerily quiet again.

I took a deep breath. Something ordinary is going on here, I told myself. Figure it out, Lauren; two people out of touch with reality is one too many.

A boat wake—that would explain the sudden movement of water. I hadn't heard a powerboat pass, but I was focused on other things; perhaps I didn't notice it. I rose to my feet.

What was Nora thinking? I wondered. That she had gotten rid of me, locking me with my mother in the boathouse?

I called out several times and received no response. I needed something heavy to bang against the door. The padlock wouldn't give way, but the old hinges might. I glanced around. Small cracks of light between the boards allowed me to orient myself. I remembered that tools had been kept in the loft and made my way slowly down the walkway. Grasping the ladder, I began to climb it, hoping none of the rungs were rotted through.

When I got to the top, I reached out gingerly. My fingers touched something metallic and small—a chain, a piece of jewelry. I tucked it in my pocket and continued to search. At last I found an object with a long handle and a cold steel end. Perfect! An ax.

I carefully backed down the ladder and felt my way to the door. Perhaps it would be smart to shout a few more times, I thought, before swinging away like Paul Bunyan.

"Hey! Let me out! Let me out!"

I waited for two minutes and screamed again. Giving up, I raised the ax, then froze when I heard someone fumbling with the lock. The door opened and I blinked at the sudden brightness.

"Well, hello," a deep voice greeted me.

"I told you to be careful," said another voice—Nick's. "There could be an ax murderer inside."

I lowered the ax and stepped into the fresh air.

Nick looked amused. "What were you doing in there?"

"Building a boat."

He laughed and turned to the man next to him. "Recognize her, Frank?"

"Barely," his uncle replied. "You've grown up, girl. You've grown up real nice. Welcome home, Lauren."

"Hey, Mr. Frank. It's good to see you again."

"Please, just Frank," he told me. "Don't make me feel any older than I am."

I grinned. His face was lined from all the sun he got and his hairline receding, but his eyes were just as bright and observant, and his smile was the same.

"How did you get locked in there?" he asked. "You couldn't have done it yourself."

"Nora helped."

Frank looked puzzled. "What do you mean?"

"She asked me to get some fishing line so she could tie up her plants."

"You mean she set you up? She trapped you?"

"Oh, come on, Frank," Nick said.

"It's hard to tell with her," I replied.

Frank shook his head. "Jule has got to get that girl some help."

"Let's not get on that subject again," Nick told his uncle.

"But it's true, Nick," I said. "Nora has become really strange."

"She's crazy," Frank declared. "One of these days she's going to do some real damage."

"She's harmless," Nick insisted.

"Sorry, kid, but she's out of touch with reality, and that's dangerous."

"Well, if she asks me to get this ax," I said, "I think I'll say no."

Frank laughed. I set the tool inside, beneath the light chain, then closed the door. Frank put the padlock on and returned the key to its hook.

"Seriously, Lauren," he went on, "you need to convince Jule to get Nora to a shrink. Jule's got to stop acting so irresponsible."

I winced; I didn't want to think the godmother I had adored for so long was anything worse than lax. But in relying on Holly to figure out how to pay the bills and denying Nora's need for help, she was letting them carry burdens that shouldn't have been theirs.

"Maybe they can't afford a doctor," Nick pointed out.

Frank's cell phone rang.

"If Jule sold that land of hers, she could afford a lot of things" he replied and plucked the phone from his pocket. "Hello. You got me. Who's this? . . . Well, is it now? How much riverfront?" He gave Nick and me a salute and headed back to his house, talking real estate and prices.

"Still making those deals," I observed.

"Seven days a week," Nick replied, walking with me along the edge of the river toward Aunt Jule's dock. "I've been painting his living room—you know

Frank, he likes cheap help—and he's been using every opportunity to talk me into a double major in business and pre-law. According to him, a law degree is better than a million lottery tickets, *if* you know how to use it."

"Meaning it's the road to riches?"

"*If* you know how to use it. He's probably afraid I'll turn out like my parents."

I laughed. Nick's father was an artist, his mother, a poet and professor at Chase, the local college. I remembered their house as a cozy shore cottage stuffed with books and smelling of linseed oil and turpentine. Nick's father and Frank had grown up in that home, the sons of a waterman with very little money. But Frank had gone on to marry a wealthy woman who owned the house and land where he now lived. She had died several years after he'd completed law school. They didn't have any children and he never remarried. Having become a prosperous lawyer and real estate developer, I guessed the only thing he had in common with Nick's parents was their love for Nick.

"So *are* you turning out like them? Do you still write and draw?"

"Yeah, but I don't do anything personal or profound. My parents take life way too seriously. I like to make people laugh. I had a regular cartoon feature in the school paper and created some for the yearbook. Social satire stuff. I've done a couple political cartoons for Wisteria's paper and just got one accepted in Easton's, which has a much bigger circulation. Impressed?" he asked, grinning.

"I am," I replied. I didn't point out that cartoons can be profound and personal, especially if he was doing political and social satire.

"So explain to me," Nick said as we walked toward the dock, "how you can ever meet guys at an all-girls school."

"There aren't a lot of chances," I admitted, "but I like it that way."

"You do? You're kidding. You have to be."

"No. We have an all-boys school nearby, and there's a regular dating exchange going. I take guys to dances, like escorts, but I don't want to date—not till I'm in college. I don't want to get hooked like my mother did and become dependent on some guy to make me feel like a person. I'm getting my life and career together first."

He looked me as if I had just landed from Mars. "That doesn't mean you can't date," he said. "I'm not getting hooked, either, and I'm dating everybody."

I laughed. "And breaking a few hearts along the way?"

He peeked sideways at me. His lashes were blond. I always knew that, but I had never thought much about his golden lashes, or his green eyes, or the way they brimmed with sunlight and laughter. Now, for some reason, this was all I could think about.

"How can you be so sure," he asked, "that *you're* not breaking hearts by not dating guys?" He turned toward me, blocking my path. "How do you know you're not breaking my heart?"

His sudden nearness took my breath away. I

stepped around him. "I'm not worried about you, just Holly, who's really looking forward to the prom."

He thought about that for a moment, then caught up with me. "I'll always be grateful to Holly," he said. "If she hadn't shown mercy, I'd be taking my mother to my last big high school event."

"What happened to all those others you're dating?" I asked.

"Well, Kelly invited me to the prom and I said yes. Then Jennifer asked me to the senior formal. And I said yes. I didn't know they were the same thing."

I laughed. "Moron!"

"Now neither of them is speaking to me, and their friends, of course, must be loyal. That kind of narrowed the playing field."

"You got what you deserved," I said, grinning. "Holly should have said no."

"Hey, does my stupidity give you the right to bruise a tender heart?"

"Yeah, yeah. I'm bruising a heart made of Play-Doh."

He laughed, then turned toward the water and whistled sharply.

I had been looking toward the house, my eyes avoiding the dock, but now I saw a dog in the river. He swam toward us, stood chest deep in the water, then came bounding forward.

"Put on your rain slicker!" Nick cried.

"What?"

The big dog stopped in front of us and shook hard, sending river water flying.

"Too late," Nick replied. "But you won't have to shower tonight. This is Rocky."

"Rocky. Hi, big guy," I said and knelt down. "Wow! What eyes!"

"Careful, he stinks, " Nick warned.

"All water retrievers do," I replied, running my hands over his thick coat. It was a rich brown and wavy. "He's a Chesapeake Bay, isn't he? His fur looks like it."

"Mostly—he's enough Chessie to swim in ice water."

"You are gorgeous!" I said, gazing into his amber eyes.

"Don't let it go to your head, Rocky," Nick told his dog. "She doesn't date."

I glanced up. "Now, a dog," I said, "that's something I miss, living at school."

"Maybe you can get an exchange going with a kennel," Nick suggested.

"No, no," I said. "I want a dog of my own to love and pamper."

Nick grunted. Rocky wagged his tail.

I petted around the dog's wet ears and scratched under his chin. "Such an intelligent face!"

"Yeah, but he's a lousy dancer."

I grinned and stood up.

"Are you headed up to the house?" Nick asked.

"Yes." As we climbed the hill, Rocky ran ahead of us, then circled back and ran ahead again. We stopped at the porch.

"You know the rules, Rock," Nick said to his dog. "No stinky animals inside."

"Are you kidding? Aunt Jule won't mind."

"I'm here to see Holly."

"Oh. Of course." She had told me he was coming. Why else did I think he was walking me to the house?

"We have yearbook work to do," Nick explained.

"At this point in the year?"

"The supplement," he answered.

"Well, Rocky can hang out with me." I stroked the dog's head. "Come on, big guy."

Rocky licked my hand and complied, walking next to me as I headed toward the side of the house.

A shrill whistle split the air. "Rocky!" Nick called, sounding exasperated. "Come here. Come!"

The dog trotted back to him.

"What's going on? You're not supposed to go off with anybody who pats you on the head. Where's your training?"

I looked back at Nick, amused. "Jealous?"

"Not of you," he replied, then motioned to the dog. "Okay, go with Lauren. Go," he commanded.

The dog raced toward me and I continued walking. With Rocky trotting beside me, I checked the greenhouse and garden in search of Nora. Though I wanted to question her about what she had done, part of me was relieved that she wasn't in either place. As strange as Nora was as a child, she had never given me the creeps. She did now. Before, when she answered someone who wasn't there, I figured it was an imaginary playmate. So what if she had one longer than most kids? But my dead mother, that was a different kind of invisible presence. I didn't want to think about it.

Passing the garden, I came to the old oak tree with

the swing. It was tied the same way as always, with a loop dangling about three feet off the ground.

"What do you think, Rocky? Am I still the champion swinger of the group?"

I grabbed the rope and gave it a hard yank, then put my foot in the loop and pulled myself up with my hands, making sure the rope was as strong as it appeared. Jumping down again, I carried the rope to another tree and climbed to "the platform of death," as we used to call it—a wide branch on an old cherry.

"Here goes." I slipped my foot in the loop, grabbed the rope, and pushed off.

With the first swoop I remembered why I had loved swinging. It was wonderful! It was flying! It was being Peter Pan! The earth fell away, the sky rushed to meet me. I was free and flying high.

Then the rope jerked. It happened so suddenly it caught me off guard. The rope writhed out of my hands. I grabbed for it frantically, but I couldn't catch hold and fell backward. With my foot caught in the loop, I hit the ground upside down, back first. The rope snapped, releasing me from the tree and tumbling on top of me.

I lay on my back stunned, the wind knocked out of me. Rocky nosed my arm. I sat up slowly and gazed up at the tree, which still had a piece of rope dangling from it. The rope had been in too good shape to be snapped by my weight. I quickly examined it, the part that had fallen on me.

About four feet above the foot loop was a knot. My mouth went dry. I thought of the knot in the lamp wire, the knots in my mother's scarves and jewelry. I had assumed that someone tied those knots before they were discovered, but I hadn't seen this one when I grasped the swing's rope.

I just didn't notice it, I told myself. Still, an icy fear ran through my veins. I didn't know how to explain what had just happened. I didn't know who or what to blame. Then I glanced up to the second floor porch and saw Nora watching me.

SIX

before I could call to her, Nora disappeared inside. I coiled up the rope and left it under the tree, then entered the house, slipping past the dining room, where Nick, Holly, and Aunt Jule were talking. When I arrived upstairs, Nora's bedroom door was closed. I could hear her moving behind it.

I knocked, lightly at first. "Nora? Nora, I want to talk to you." I knocked harder, but she wouldn't answer. I thought of opening the door myself or sneaking around to the porch and trying to surprise her, but I didn't want to do something to Nora that she could do back to me. I gave up. As soon as I got a chance to talk to Aunt Jule alone, I'd tell her that Nora needed help and I'd offer to pay for it.

After changing out of my grass-stained clothes, I took a paperback from the bedroom shelf and joined the others in the dining room. Aunt Jule was working on her embroidery. Nick and Holly had cleared space on the table and laid out piles of photos. They were going through them, laughing and arguing, as they did years back when playing board games. I threw some pillows in the corner of the room and curled up to read the battered Agatha Christie the way I used to read Aunt Jule's Nancy Drews. It was almost like old times.

After a while Rocky was admitted as far as the hallway door. Stretching out next to him, I continued to read. Once, when I looked up, I found Nick staring at Rocky and me, smiling.

Holly glanced up. "Phew!" she exclaimed, waving a folder in front of her nose.

"Shh!" Nick said in a stage whisper. "You'll embarrass Lauren. Just make sure she showers tonight."

"I was referring to Rocky."

Aunt Jule laughed. I saw the same content look on her face as she'd get when we gathered around her as children.

Nora came in twice and stayed no longer than five minutes each time. She would eye me warily, then sit by Nick. He was gentle with her, showing her a handful of pictures and asking which ones she'd choose for the yearbook supplement. Now that I thought about it, she had always sat near him when we played board games and defended his claims against Holly's.

Nick stayed through dinnertime, not that there was an event called dinner at Aunt Jule's. We simply helped ourselves to what we wanted, when we wanted it. About ten o'clock Holly walked Nick to his car. I couldn't help wondering if they were outside kissing.

Since tonight wasn't an official date but a yearbook meeting, I figured his policy conveniently allowed for as many of these nights as he wanted.

"Lauren," Aunt Jule said when we were alone, "I was hoping we'd have time together tomorrow after Holly leaves for school—to chat and all. But I have a shop-keeper breathing down my neck for overdue work and have to pick up craft supplies. I'll be gone till noon."

"No problem," I assured her.

"I could meet you at twelve," she offered, "and go with you to Sondra's grave. We could take flowers. If you like, we could plant some."

I knew she was trying to make up for what she had said before.

"Thanks, Aunt Jule, thanks a lot, but I need to go by myself." I walked over and sat on the chair next to hers. "But there is something I want to talk to you about."

She paused, holding her silver needle above the fabric she was embroidering. "Yes, love?"

"Nora."

She quickly pushed the needle through. "What about her?"

"I'm really worried about her. I think she needs help—psychiatric help."

"Do you," Aunt Jule replied coolly.

"This afternoon Nora—"

"Nick told us about the boathouse," my godmother interrupted. "It was a childish prank. Certainly you weren't frightened by such a silly thing?"

"I was bothered by the way she talked about my mother. She said—"

"Ignore her," Aunt Jule advised, making a knot and snipping the thread. "Nora is confused and easily frightened, especially when there are changes here at home. Your visit has upset her a little, that's all. She'll get past it. In the meantime, don't take her seriously."

"But what if she wants to be taken seriously?" I asked. "What if her behavior is a cry for help?"

Aunt Jule shook her head, dismissing the possibility. "You're tired, Lauren, and so am I. This isn't the time to discuss Nora. Get a good night's rest and let things settle for a few days."

"Is Nora the reason you asked me to come here?" I persisted. "Is she what you wanted to talk about?"

"There is much for us to talk about, *after* you've rested up," Aunt Jule replied firmly.

I knew that once my godmother tabled a discussion, it was useless to say more. I kissed her good night.

When I got upstairs, Nora's bedroom door was closed. Before entering my own room, I glanced at the door across the hall, next to Nora's. The summer my mother came, she had slept in that room. I was glad the door to it was also shut.

In my room I turned on a small lamp and lay back on my bed for a moment, listening to the familiar night sounds. A breeze wafted in through the screen door, pushing back the light curtains. I reached lazily into my shorts pocket to remove my car keys. My fingers felt something else—the chain I'd found in the boathouse.

I had forgotten all about it. I sat up quickly and opened my hand. The necklace was so black that for a moment I didn't recognize the small tarnished heart.

When I did, I couldn't believe it. I had thought it was gone forever!

The silver necklace was a gift from Aunt Jule when I was born. I had loved it and worn it at the shore every summer, though on a sturdier chain than the original. The summer my mother had come, she had taken it from me after a fight with Aunt Jule. The next day I had sneaked into her room and searched for the necklace everywhere—her jewelry case and purse, her bureau drawers and suitcase. I didn't find it and feared she had done as she'd threatened—thrown it in the river.

So how had it ended up in the loft? Though the boathouse was in better shape seven years ago, I couldn't imagine my mother going in, much less hiding something there. But if Aunt Jule, Nora, or Holly had found the necklace, why wasn't it returned to me? Maybe they meant to, but forgot. A lot of things went undone and forgotten around here. Still, why keep it in the boathouse loft?

I hung the necklace on the wood post of my mirror stand, puzzling over the events of the day. I had come here to tie up my memories like a box of old photos, so I could put them away once and for all. But the memories would not be neatly bound up; questions kept unraveling.

I didn't know what time it was or where I was, except far beneath the surface of a river. The river bottom was thick with sea grass and I swam in near darkness. Someone called my name, *Laur-en, Laur-en,* the voice rising and falling over the syllables as my mother's once had.

I followed the voice, swimming through the long weed, feeling it flow over my skin like cold tentacles.

"Lauren! Lauren!" It *was* my mother. She was panicking.

I swam harder, trying to find her. I needed air, but somehow I continued scouring the bottom. The sea grass wrapped itself around my arms and legs, entangling me.

"Lauren, come quickly!"

I broke free and kept swimming. I could feel her fear as if it were my own. I knew she was sinking into a place where I couldn't reach her, an endless night.

The banks of the river narrowed. Both sides were walls of tree roots, roots like long, arthritic fingers reaching out to catch me. I fought my way through them. But as her voice grew near, the river walls pressed closer together, threatening to swallow me alive.

"Where are you?" I cried out.

"Here."

Ahead of me was a deep crack where the two banks joined, a long and jagged fissure.

"Here, Lauren," she called out from the fissure. "Lauren, dearest, come to Mother."

But I didn't want to go where she was. I hesitated, and the crack closed, sealing her in forever.

I woke up sweating. My heart pounded and I gulped air as if I were emerging from deep water.

Laur-en.

I turned my head toward the hall, thinking I heard the same voice. Silence.

I climbed out of bed and tiptoed to the door. When

I opened it, the door to my mother's old room creaked. Someone had left it ajar.

I crossed the hall and laid my palms against the door, listening a moment, then pushed it open. At the other end of the room a glass door to the porch suddenly closed. I started toward it and the door behind me slammed shut.

I screamed, then muffled it. A draft, I told myself, a draft running through my room and this one blew the doors shut. I wondered if it had been caused by someone making a hasty exit through the porch door.

I strode across the room, opened the doors to the porch, and leaned out. No one was there. Of course, if it had been Nora, she could have easily slipped into her room, the next door down.

Inside, I turned on the floor lamp and glanced around. It looked as I remembered it, with oak furniture similar to my own and a red-and-green quilt on the bed. Spiders had made themselves cozy here and dust coated the bureau top, but the dresser had streaks on its surface, as if someone had been using it recently. One of its drawers wasn't closed all the way.

I walked over and opened it. Inside were several old newspapers, tabloids that were badly yellowed. I spread them out on the dresser top. I guessed what was in them; still, the pictures of my mother shocked me— those horrible flashbulb photos that could make the prettiest woman look like a witch.

Had she put them here? Not unless she wanted to torture herself, I thought. The only other thing in the drawer was an empty packet of marigold seeds.

I opened the next drawer. My mother's favorite pair of earrings lay on top of a scarf she had loved. I touched them gently. At the town house in Washington, my mother's personal things had been put in safe storage or thrown out soon after she died. I still had her jewelry box in my room at school, but it seemed like mine now more than hers. These items were different—barely touched by anyone else. I half-expected to smell her perfume on them.

In the corner of the drawer were snippets of photographs. For a moment I couldn't figure out what I was looking at, then I saw they were pictures from that last summer, with my mother cut out. Not exactly subtle symbolism, I thought. In the third drawer there were more empty seed packets and a pile of plant catalogs that had been mailed to Nora.

Were all these things Nora's? Some of the garden catalogs were dated the summer of the current year, which meant Nora had opened the bureau recently; it wasn't as if she had forgotten these things were here. I found it unsettling to think that anyone would keep the rag-paper photos of my mother seven years after her death. Equally disturbing was the possibility that, after all this time, Nora could have mimicked perfectly the intonation of my mother's voice. This was the behavior of someone obsessed with a person, obsessed with a dead woman.

I left everything as I'd found it, planning to show it to Aunt Jule, then turned out the light and left.

"Is everything all right?"

"Holly!" I hadn't expected her to be in the hall.

Nora stood behind Holly, her dark eyes glittering in the soft light. I was too tired to confront her now and wasn't sure I'd get anywhere if I did. The person to talk to was Aunt Jule.

"Everything's fine," I answered Holly.

"Are you sure?"

"I had a bad dream and got up to walk around—to shake it off—that's all."

Holly turned her head, glancing sideways at her sister, as if suspicious of something more, then said, "Nora, go to bed."

Nora moved past her sister and peeked into the room from which I had just come.

"Nora," Holly said quietly but firmly. Nora returned to her bedroom.

Holly guided me into mine. "You look upset," she observed as she turned on the lamp. "Do you want to talk?"

"Thanks, but it's awfully late," I replied.

"I'm wide awake," she assured me, sitting on my bed. She must have wondered what was going on, especially if she heard my muffled scream.

"Nick told us Nora locked you in the boathouse," Holly continued. "I don't know what to say, Lauren, except I'm sorry it happened. Please don't take it personally."

"What if it was meant personally?"

"Just do your best to avoid her," Holly advised. "And next time Nora starts making trouble for you, tell me. Someone has to keep tabs on her. Since Mom doesn't, I'm the warden of this asylum."

"Holly, what's going to happen to Nora when you go away to college?"

"I don't even want to think about it," she said. "But Nora is a long-term problem. Right now I'm more concerned about you. It has to be hard coming back and seeing things you associate with your mother's death."

I glanced away. "I thought that by now it would be easier, but I was wrong."

She rested her hand lightly on my shoulder. "Then tell me what I can do to help, okay? I'm not in your shoes, so I can't guess."

"Okay."

She stood up. "Well, get some sleep. Tomorrow will be better."

"Right. G'night."

After Holly left, I locked my door to the hall and latched the screen doors to the porch. It felt strange, for I had never worried about my own safety at Aunt Jule's.

Reaching for the switch on my bureau lamp, I noticed that my newfound necklace was twisted up. I touched it with one finger, expecting it to swing free from the mirror stand, but it didn't. Like my mother's necklaces, it had been tied in impossible knots.

seven

I didn't fall back asleep until dawn. Waking late on Monday morning, I found myself alone in the house. Two notes had been left on the fridge for me, one from Aunt Jule reminding me that she'd be out till twelve, and the other from Holly. She invited me to stop by the yearbook office so she could introduce me to her friends. The underclassmen were on a half-day schedule, so she suggested I come at noon.

A list of needed grocery and household items was also on the refrigerator door. When I tucked it in my purse I discovered a second note from Holly that contained a log of bills due and overdue, adding up to a cool $4,000. I knew that dropping a big check wouldn't solve the problem—Aunt Jule would continue to be Aunt Jule. But it would relieve the pressure for the time being and give Holly an easier summer before college.

When I left the house Nora was in the knot garden

snipping a boxwood hedge with hand clippers. The square garden, started in the 1800s, was once an intricate green design of shrubs, herbs, and colored gravel. When I was a child it had grown into one large mass of green. But Nora must have been cutting back the shrubs little by little each year. Now they looked like lumpy green caterpillars and were starting to trace out a pattern.

"Good morning," I called to her.

She looked across the outer hedge but said nothing.

"I'm doing some errands," I told her. "Do you need anything?"

"No."

I watched her work for a moment. "Nora, why did you lock me in the boathouse yesterday?"

She raked the top of the boxwood with her fingers, brushing off the fresh clippings. "I don't remember."

"Why did you run from it? What did you see?"

"I don't remember," she insisted.

"The water was stirred up," I reminded her, "as if a boat were passing by. Did you notice a powerboat?"

Nora shook her head. "It was her. She was making the river angry. She wants to make the river come up."

"Who?" I asked, though I could guess the answer.

"Sondra. She wants it to go over our heads."

"No, Nora, it was just—"

"She wants to pull us down with her," Nora said, her eyes wide, as if she were seeing something I couldn't. "She wants her little girl."

I gripped my car keys hard. "Listen to me. There is no one sleeping in there, dead or alive."

Nora's eyelids twitched violently.

"Wind, tides, boats," I said, "those are the things that make the water rise and fall."

She didn't reply.

"Nora, while I'm out I'm going to visit my mother's grave. She was buried in the cemetery at Grace Church—by the high school. My mother is not in the river. She's not in the boathouse. She's in a grave in the churchyard. The stone has her name on it to tell you that's where she is. Do you understand? Do you hear me?"

She turned away and resumed clipping the hedge.

There was no reaching her, no way I knew of. She needed professional help.

I continued on to my car, stopping at the big oak to look at the swing's rope, which I had left coiled beneath. I studied the knot, then touched it timidly. There was nothing unusual about it. It must have been there all along and I just hadn't noticed.

It was a quick drive to the bank. High Street had been swept clean after the festival and basked quietly in the morning sunshine. Its main bank was a small-town miniature of the kind you see in East Coast cities, with bronze doors and Greek columns. I think the teller I got must have been there since it was built. Her fluffy white hair flew in the breeze made by a little desk fan. Pursing her lips, she read my check and driver's license, then lifted her head to study me, pushing her heavy glasses up her nose, so she could get a clearer view.

"Sondra's daughter."

"Yes," I said.

"You're depositing this in the Ingram account."

I realized that teens didn't usually write a check as large as mine. "Here's my bankbook," I told her, sliding it under the glass. "It has phone numbers and an e-mail address if you want to verify the availability of the money."

"No. Your mama's checks were always good," she said.

I nodded, though I didn't know what she was talking about. My mother didn't bank here.

"And always on time," she added as she started the transaction. "The first of each month Jule would come in to deposit them."

I looked at the teller with surprise.

"I always wondered why," the woman continued. "Of course, I figured your mama was being black-mailed, but I wondered what for."

Blackmailed? I stared at the woman.

"When I told that to folks here at the bank, they laughed."

Small wonder, I thought.

"When I told the police, they said I read too many paperbacks. But the real reason they didn't believe me was Jule. She's golden around here. The Ingram family, they're like the Scarboroughs, Wisteria's royalty."

"I see."

"Just between you and me," the teller said, peering at me, her eyes magnified by her glasses, "why *was* your mama paying off Jule?"

"She was just helping out," I replied, "like I'm doing."

The old woman gazed at me doubtfully.

I wondered if my mother had been in the habit of lending money to Aunt Jule, and if my godmother had become dependent on her. I knew my mother was good at manipulating others with her wealth—I'd heard my father tell her that more than once. Perhaps money was the cause of her and Aunt Jule's arguments that summer.

The teller stamped my check and handed me a receipt. As I turned to leave, I heard raised voices in one of the bank's offices. A door with frosted glass swung open and Frank emerged, his face red with anger. He didn't see me and, given his scarlet color and indignant gait, I thought he might not want me to see him. I turned aside and took my time putting my bankbook away, mulling over what I had learned from the teller.

My mother and godmother had been best friends since their middle-school years at Birch Hill and probably had known each other's deepest secrets. But the teller's suggestion of blackmail was absurd. So was my idea that my mother was controlling my godmother with money, for Aunt Jule had nothing to offer her in return.

Besides, my mother had loved Aunt Jule. In the will Frank had drawn up for my mother that summer, she had left her entire estate to me, to be inherited at the age of eighteen. But if I died before then, my inheritance was to go to Aunt Jule. Obviously my mother trusted her; there was no reason for me to doubt their relationship now.

"Lauren, you found us," Holly said, sounding pleased. "Everyone, this is Lauren Brandt."

Kids looked up from two rows of computer screens, greeting me with a chorus of hellos. Nick sat at a drawing table fifteen feet away, ink on his fingers and balled-up sheets of paper ringing his chair. He flashed me one of those smiles a girl could believe was just for her; I was smart enough not to. I tried to spread my smile to him and those around him, then turned to Holly.

"You look like you're busy. I'll come by at a better time."

"No, no, stay," she replied. "Karen, would you show Lauren around the office, introduce her to people, and tell her what's going on?"

A girl pushed back from her desk, tucked a strand of hair behind her ear, and obliged. I felt self-conscious, like I was playing my father touring a factory. Nick looked across the room at me and winked.

The walls of the yearbook room were covered with schedules, posters, photos of school events, and cartoons—Nick's, I figured. My father was the star of several of his pieces. In the cartoon that hung above Nick's table, my dad's tooth-filled smile bloomed over a podium as he announced, "I promise to lead Maryland in the Industrial Evolution." Smokestacks rose in the background; three-legged frogs and two-headed geese applauded.

Nick caught me studying it, and I quickly glanced away. When I looked back, he turned away, both of us pretending that I hadn't noticed the drawing.

Holly saw us and her hand flew up to her mouth. "Oh, Lauren, I'm sorry."

"Don't worry about it," I replied, moving on hurriedly to sports photos.

"I didn't even think about it," she explained. "After a while, you forget what's hanging up."

Everyone in the room started checking the walls to see what was hanging up.

"No problem," I assured her.

Holly bit her lip and looked at Nick. So did everyone else, figuring out that it was something of his. Luckily, a guy with funky red hair and a lot of freckles came in right then and saved me from further embarrassment.

"Well, boys and girls, I'm back from the Queen," he announced loudly, then threw himself down in a chair as if he'd just swum the distance from England. "Got it all scoped out," he told Holly.

She turned to him, and Karen filled me in: "Our prom is tonight at the Queen Victoria Hotel. Steve's a photographer."

"So give me a list of your shots," Holly said to Steve.

"They're in my head."

"Put them on paper," she told him. "How's the entrance looking?"

"Very rosy," he replied, leaning back in his chair. "It clashes with my hair, but then, I'm not part of the scene."

"You mean it's red?" Holly exclaimed. "I told them to make the archway white or pastel."

"That's what happens when you're not running everything," he remarked. I heard a muffled laugh in the corner of the room.

"But we need contrast for the photos," she insisted. "I told them that. They'll be sorry when they see their spread."

"There's always Adobe Photoshop," Nick suggested.

"Yes, of course," Holly replied, "but that will take time."

Nick smiled at her. "I was joking, Holly. This is a yearbook. We're supposed to be preserving memories, not creating them."

"Some people just don't get it," she said. "Well, I warned them." She leaned back against a desk and drummed her fingers.

"Listen, Holly," I interrupted, "I have a few more things to do."

She hopped up. "I'll walk you out." When we got outside the room, she asked, "So, how's it going today?"

"Pretty good."

"Have you visited your mom's grave yet?"

"That's where I'm going next," I replied.

"Want me to go with you?"

I was surprised and touched by her offer. "Thanks, but no."

"I've got time," she told me. "The cemetery is right across the street. Don't get snowed by my busy editor-in-chief act. It just makes me feel important," she added, laughing. "Why don't I go?"

"Thanks, but this time I'd rather be by myself."

She studied me for a moment, then nodded. "Okay."

"Oh, and I transferred the money."

She grabbed my hand. "You're a lifesaver!"

"So I'll see you at home." I turned to walk away.

"Holly," one of the kids called from inside. "Holly, tell Lauren to wait. We've got a great idea!"

Holly raised an eyebrow at me, then stuck her head through the door.

"We're going to fix her up with Jason," a girl said. "What do you think?"

Holly was quiet for a moment, then smiled. "I think it's brilliant."

"They'll look good under the arch, red roses or not," the photographer needled.

Holly ignored him. "I'll dig up a dress for you, Lauren, so don't worry about that. Shoes, too. One of us will have something from last year that'll work." To the group she announced, "I'm taking one-night donations—formals and shoes."

"Whoa! Wait a minute, what are we talking about?" I said, stepping into the doorway.

Karen, my guide, pointed to a photo of a great-looking guy in a basketball uniform. "Jason Deere. Star forward for W.H., just ditched by his yearlong girlfriend. He needs a date for tonight's prom."

"Well, thanks, but I'm busy," I said.

"Doing what?" Holly asked. "Come on, Lauren. It will be good for you."

"It will be better for Jason," Nick observed.

I glanced at him.

"You date, don't you?" Nick asked with a sly smile.

"I go to dances."

"What's Jason's cell-phone number?" a guy hollered.

"Wait a minute," I protested.

He picked up the phone and someone called out a number.

I didn't want to talk to some guy I had never met in front of a room full of people.

"If he wants to, fine," I told Holly, walking away as fast as I could. "Tell me when you get home."

Just before the hall's double doors closed between

us, she gave me the thumbs-up sign and called out, "I'll pick up an extra boutonniere."

My car was parked on the church side of Scarborough Road. I stopped there just long enough to open the trunk and throw in my purse, then followed a brick path that led past the church to the cemetery beside it. Grace Presbyterian, built in the 1800s, had a deep sloping roof and a simple bell tower on one corner. On a sunny day its graveyard, shaded by a huge copper beech and tall, lacy cedars, felt ten degrees cooler than the street.

My mother had been buried here because Aunt Jule had said it was her wish. The day of the funeral I'd been too upset to notice anything about her plot, including where it was. I knew the church office would have a map for locating graves, but I wandered up and down the rows, reading names and dates. The dappled light fell gently on stones smoothed by decades of rain. Old trees rustled soft as angel wings. I suddenly felt hot tears in my eyes. If only my mother could have known this kind of peace when she was alive.

At last I came upon her grave, a polished granite stone, and knelt in the grass beside it. For a moment I hurt so much I couldn't breathe. My heart felt squeezed into a small, sharp rock. Then the feeling passed. I wiped away tears I hadn't realized I was shedding.

I sagged back against the marker next to my mother's. How cold these stones felt on a summer day, I thought. I ran my fingers over her name, then turned to see who was lying next to her, for the marker was very close. It was pink granite and slightly smaller than hers.

DAUGHTER, I read.

Daughter! Me! This was to be my grave.

I felt as I did when I was a child—smothered by her. It was just like her, not caring who else might be in my life, counting on my coming back to her.

When had she made these arrangements? I wondered. When she wrote the new will? That had been a week or two before she died.

A terrifying idea crept into my mind. What if my mother's fears were not as groundless as we had thought? What if someone really had been after her and she, with no one to believe or protect her, had made these preparations?

That's crazy, I told myself, rising to my feet, heading back to the car. There was another explanation for the grave. My mother had given birth to me here, having left my father for a time and run to the sanctuary of Aunt Jule's arms. Perhaps she had made the arrangements then.

When I reached my car, I retrieved my purse from the trunk, then opened the driver-side door. A sheet of white paper lay folded on the front seat. I gazed at it, puzzled, until I realized I had left my window cracked for air. Someone must have slipped the paper through. I picked up the note and flipped it open. The message, written in block letters, was simple: YOU'RE NEXT.

eight

I spun around to see if someone was watching from behind, then quickly surveyed the street, church lawn, and school area. Several groups of kids lingered on the school steps. Two people dressed like teachers leaned on a parked car, talking. No one appeared to be interested in me.

I stared at the note. Was it just a prank or a warning to be taken seriously? Was it Nora's?

She knew I was coming here, but then so did Aunt Jule and Holly, and I wasn't eager to blame either of them. Perhaps I was being unfair to Nora. Perhaps, but Aunt Jule and Holly hadn't locked me in the boathouse. They didn't keep a cache of my mother's things and didn't silently stand by as I fell from a swing.

I refolded the note and placed it in my purse.

When we were children, Nora had been a gentle friend; I could easily believe she was harmless—harmless

in her heart. But people act according to how they see
the world outside them, and she saw it in a very distorted way. In her mental state, would she understand
the real-life consequences of her actions? Had Nora
pushed my mother in anger and watched her float in
the river, not comprehending the finality of what she
had done until it was too late?

If that were true, I'd learn to come to grips with it
and accept that Nora wasn't mentally responsible. But
that wasn't the only thing troubling me now. How did
Nora see me? What if I were an unnerving reminder of
my mother and she needed to get rid of me, too, without comprehending all of what that meant?

I was more shaken than I realized—it took several
tries to insert my key in the ignition. At the grocery
store I had to check and recheck my list, unable to con-
centrate on the task. When I finally arrived home, I
didn't see Nora in the garden or greenhouse. I called for
her in the house but it was Aunt Jule who responded,
saying she was somewhere outside.

Aunt Jule eyed the bags I'd hauled into the kitchen.
"Good lord, what have you done?"

"Picked up some things."

"You didn't have to do that, Lauren."

"I wanted to," I said, and began to put the groceries
away. "Is Holly home yet?"

"No, after yearbook stuff she has a manicure
appointment." Aunt Jule helped unpack the bags, setting boxes randomly on shelves, placing soap powder
between instant potatoes and tea. "Tonight's the prom,
you know."

I nodded.

"So what do you think of Nick?" she asked.

"Some of those boxes are upside down," I pointed out.

"Honestly, you're as compulsive as Holly," she said. "Soon you'll be reminding me to turn off the lights." Then she smiled slyly. "Or maybe you're just wiggling out of my question. What do you think of the grown-up Nick?"

"He's gotten taller."

"He's gotten terrifically handsome," she said. "And either you're blind or you're faking it."

I laughed. "There's no need for you to be shopping guys for me, Aunt Jule. I stopped by to see Holly and was drafted to go to the prom with some jock—one that's terrifically handsome, as you'd say."

"You were always such cute little pals, you and Nick," Aunt Jule went on. "I loved watching you play together. You were friends from the start."

"It's nice to see that Holly and he are good friends now," I replied, reminding her of Holly's interest.

She nodded without enthusiasm, then picked up a basket of fresh strawberries and poured them into a colander.

"Listen, Aunt Jule, we really do need to talk about Nora. She needs psychiatric help."

My godmother carried the colander to the sink, turning her back on me.

"She needs it now."

"That's your opinion," Aunt Jule replied as she washed the berries.

"And Holly's, and Frank's. Frank says Nora is out of touch with reality and that it's dangerous. He said one of these days she's going to—"

"If you ask me, people out of touch with reality aren't nearly as dangerous as lawyers like him who manipulate it."

"At least have her evaluated by a professional," I pleaded, "then we can decide from there."

"We? You've become quite the grown-up, Lauren," she observed.

"I meant *you*. But I'll pay for it."

"How nice of you!" she replied sarcastically.

I was baffled by her attitude.

She shook the water hard from the colander of berries. "You stay away for seven years, Lauren, and after one day back, you start telling me how to fix things. You're here for twenty-four hours and you're cocksure you know what Nora needs."

"All I'm saying is get her checked out. If a doctor says she needs treatment, I'll pay for it, all of it."

"Will you now? Sometimes, Lauren, you act just like Sondra, believing your money makes you superior, using your money to make other people do what *you* think they should do."

"I care about Nora! I'm trying to help her!"

"You're just like Sondra," Aunt Jule went on, "deciding how other people should lead their lives, deciding what's normal, what isn't, what's to be admired, what's to be scorned. There are more ways to do it than *your* way."

"But—"

"You walk like Sondra. You talk like Sondra. I *hate* it when you act like her."

The bitterness I heard in Aunt Jule's voice amazed me. I felt torn between insisting that I wasn't like my mother—I had tried hard not to be—and defending her.

"Well, there is one thing my mother and I share," I told her. "Nora's intense dislike for us."

My godmother twisted plastic bags in her hands, then balled them up.

"Aunt Jule, have you ever thought about the fact that it was Nora who summoned us, Nora who said she found my mother floating in the water?"

I steeled myself, figuring my godmother would be furious at what I was suggesting, but she answered with a flick of her hand. "Of course I have. Sondra's reckless death traumatized Nora as well as you, and I still haven't forgiven her for that."

I realized then that Aunt Jule would never consider the possibility that her daughter was responsible in some way. Pressing the issue wouldn't bring my mother back or get Nora the help she needed.

"Last night, after I was asleep, I thought I heard someone calling my name, calling it the same way my mother did. The door to the room where my mother had stayed was ajar and I went in. I found old tabloid pictures of her in the dresser, photos from that summer, her earrings, and her scarf, mixed in with items that belonged to Nora. Why would Nora have these things? Why would she think my mother is in the river or asleep in the boathouse? Don't you see? She is obsessed with her. She needs—"

"Perhaps you're the one obsessed," Aunt Jule countered icily, "hearing Sondra's voice calling you, reading into insignificant comments. It's time to move on, Lauren, and clearly you haven't."

I wouldn't give up. "Nora and I used to play together. We used to be friends. Why does she hate me now?"

"She doesn't hate you."

"Why does she act the way she does?" I persisted.

"Because you've grown into Sondra," Aunt Jule replied, tight-lipped.

I looked her straight in the eye. "I don't think so."

We turned away from each other and worked silently for a minute.

"Aunt Jule, why did you stop the police from doing a full investigation?"

"I'm sorry," she replied, setting down a bag of sugar, "I don't think I heard you right, Lauren."

I knew she had. "It would have been better to let them investigate my mother's death so we could rule out everything but an accident."

"You ungrateful brat! I was protecting you!"

She stalked out the porch door and slammed it shut. I stood quietly for several minutes, staring down at the cans I held, then continued to put things away. The tears were there again, burning my eyes, but I didn't let them fall.

I spent an hour in my room, untying the tiny knots in my necklace, polishing the silver links and tarnished heart. I had seen Aunt Jule angry before—furious the summer my mother came—but her anger had never been directed at me, not until now. I felt as if I were reliving my mother's stay here seven years ago.

I didn't see Nora that afternoon, but I didn't look for her, either. About five o'clock I took a walk and watched storm clouds mounting over the bay. Dinner was a sandwich alone in the kitchen. I didn't know if Aunt Jule was still angry at me or simply wary after the argument. Returning to my room, I heard the radio in hers, but I didn't stop by.

About six-thirty Holly knocked on my door, then entered, wiggling her fingers.

I admired her nails. "Fabulous!" I said.

"Fake," she replied, "but what the heck. I put the boutonnieres in the fridge. Do you know how many girls would like to go to the prom with Jason?"

"Well, if anyone wants to take my place . . ." I began.

"Cut it out. You want the bathroom first? I've got to make sure these are dry."

"Sure."

"I'll hang your dress on the closet door. You've got a pile of shoes to choose from."

"Thanks for getting all that together."

"Glad to," she replied. "This is going to be great!"

When I returned from the bathroom twenty minutes later, I found the shoe boxes piled neatly and the dress hanging on the door. One look told me the gown wouldn't fit, though it would have been perfect for Holly with her tall model-like frame. I figured it was hers—its blue matched her eyes.

"Jason had better not be picky about his last-minute dates," I muttered as I unzipped the back.

When I put on the dress, I didn't know whether to laugh or cry; a sleeping bag would have been as flattering. I gathered the waist with my fingers, trying to shorten the dress and give it some shape, then padded down the hall toward Aunt Jule's room to find something I could tie around me as a belt. I hoped she was in a better mood.

"Good Lord!" she exclaimed before I could say a word. "Are you trying to be nominated for wallflower of the year?"

"I thought a belt might help."

She clucked and came toward me. "It's going to need more than that," she said, grasping the fabric, lifting the dress up from my shoulders. "Perhaps your date can bring football pads."

"I think he plays basketball."

"Then we'll have to use his shoes."

I laughed, glad to know she was back to her old self.

With her hands still on my shoulders, she turned me around, then shook her head. "I don't know why Holly thought her dress would fit you. Let's see what I've got. I may have to do some fast sewing."

I followed her into the walk-in closet, a pleasantly chaotic room, where Nora, Holly, and I used to play. Aunt Jule suddenly seized on something. "This is it! Perfect. Halter tops never go out of style, not when you have pretty shoulders."

She pulled out a rather slinky red dress.

"Wow."

"I *was* pretty *wow,*" she said, "back in the days when I could fit in this. Now you can be."

"I don't know," I said, touching the stretchy red fabric.

She marched me out of the closet and turned me toward the mirror. "Lauren, look at yourself. Do you really want to go to a prom looking like you're playing dress-ups?"

I shook my head.

"So give it a try. Don't be prim."

"I'm not prim," I argued. "I just don't want to call attention to myself, and red does."

"So does a dress several sizes too big."

"True."

"How about shoes?" Aunt Jule asked.

"Holly brought me several pairs."

"Do they fit as well as her dress?"

"I haven't tried them yet."

Aunt Jule disappeared inside the closet. Box lids started flying. "Here we are."

She emerged holding up a pair of red heels. "Okay," she said, noting the expression on my face, "so they're retro. Trust me, when guys see you in these, they'll be falling all over you."

"Or I'll be falling all over them. How can you stand in heels that tall and skinny? I've got four-inchers, but they're not on pinpoints."

"Try them," she said.

I did, walking back and forth in my room, then up and down the porch, my heels clicking loudly, my bathrobe blowing in the breeze of arriving storms.

At eight-fifteen I was dressed and surveyed myself in the mirror once more. The red gown was the most

sophisticated thing I'd ever worn. The slits up its sides
did more than provide a view of my legs, they were
necessary if I wanted to walk rather than hop like the
Easter Bunny.

I picked up the little evening bag Aunt Jule had lent
me and headed downstairs. When I reached the lower
hall, I heard Frank, Holly, and Aunt Jule talking. I
assumed the guys hadn't arrived yet. Relaxing a little, I
entered the river room and strode toward the fireplace,
where Holly was posing.

Frank glanced over his shoulder, then turned around
and whistled at me.

"Really, Frank!" Aunt Jule said, but this once he had
succeeded in pleasing her.

Holly looked at me with surprise. "Where did you
get that dress?"

"It's your mom's."

"I lent you mine," she said.

"It was beautiful, but it didn't fit."

"Surely, Holly," Aunt Jule interjected, "a girl into
details, as you are, would have noticed that you and
Lauren are built very differently."

I heard the put-down in my godmother's voice and
wished she'd act more like a mother and less like a
goading sister.

"Holly, you look incredible," I said. She was wearing a
silk dress that perfectly matched her sapphire eyes. Her
long black hair swept down over thin straps and a low-
cut back. "I want a picture of you for my room at school."

"Perhaps one of you gals together," Frank suggested.

"No," Holly said. "With our dates and individually."

I didn't argue. It was her prom, we should do what she wanted. I backed up and sat down on a hassock. With the height of my shoes and the low seat, my knees shot up. So did the tight skirt, its slit climbing three quarters of the way up my leg.

"I don't know about these shoes, Aunt Jule," I said. "You could use them for hole punchers."

A deep laugh sounded behind me. I jumped.

"Nick! I didn't know you were here."

"I came in from the porch," he said.

He looked terrific and surprisingly at ease in his tux.

"Why didn't you say something?"

His green eyes held mine for a moment, shining softly. "I couldn't think of anything."

"That's rather unusual for you, Nick," Aunt Jule remarked.

Frank agreed with a grunt.

Nick smiled and sat in the chair behind me. "Enjoy it while it lasts." His eyes dropped down to my legs.

I pulled on my dress, then self-consciously rested my hand on my calf. Nick watched Holly pose but kept stealing glances at my legs. I couldn't stand it, the funny, fluttery feelings I was getting whenever he looked at me. I turned to face him. "This is nothing new," I said quietly. "You've seen both my legs before."

He leaned closer. "Then why are you covering them up?"

"Okay, next beauty," Frank announced.

I looked up and discovered Holly glaring at us. I couldn't blame her.

"It's not my prom, Frank," I said. "I don't want any

pictures of me." What I really didn't want was to draw attention away from Holly.

"Well, your godmother might. Jule?"

"Yes, definitely," she said.

I stood up reluctantly.

While Frank was taking my picture, Nora walked in and sat on the floor next to Nick.

"Hey, Nora girl," Frank greeted her.

She didn't respond.

"Frank, I want one of Lauren and me together," Aunt Jule said. "She looks so grown-up, so very beautiful."

Nora turned her head. Her eyes studied every detail of me, making me uneasy.

"And then how about some pictures of Aunt Jule with Nora, and Aunt Jule with Holly," I suggested.

"No, we have plenty of us already," my godmother replied, standing next to me, putting her arm around me. "You look absolutely stunning, love. You'll be the belle of the ball."

I stole a look at Holly, who, luckily, didn't seem to be listening. She and Nick were going down a checklist for the yearbook's coverage of the prom.

Aunt Jule and I smiled at Frank's command, then she suddenly bent her head close to mine, studying the chain around my neck. "You're wearing it!" she exclaimed. "The heart I gave you when you were a baby. I didn't know you still had it."

Holly glanced up.

"Look, girls," Aunt Jule said, lifting the pendant with one finger. "It's the little heart I gave Lauren. Do you remember it?"

Nora shook her head no.

"I think so," Holly said. "Is it gold?"

"Silver," Aunt Jule replied.

"I don't remember," Nora said.

"Of course you do," Aunt Jule insisted. "Lauren wore it all the time. She'd get a white mark on her little sun-tanned neck. Sondra took it from you, Lauren," Aunt Jule recalled. "I was so afraid she had gotten rid of it. Where did you find it?"

"Don't tell," Nora said.

"In the boathouse."

"Don't tell! It's a secret!" Nora cried out.

Aunt Jule and Holly turned to her, both of them frowning.

"Sondra wants the little heart," Nora went on. "Sondra will get it back."

Frank shook his head and sent Nick a knowing look.

"Nora, Sondra is dead," Nick said quietly.

The doorbell rang.

"Who's next?" Nora asked.

"That's Lauren's date," Holly replied sharply. "Now, keep quiet! Try to act normal and not embarass us all."

Nora bit her lip and turned to Nick. He laid his hand on her shoulder. "Everything's all right." The expression on his face, the sound of his voice, was heartbreakingly gentle.

But it was my heart that had been broken the night my mother died, not Nora's, and everything wasn't all right.

nine

The doorbell rang for the third time.

"What do you think," Frank asked, "should we let in Lauren's date before he tries another house?"

Nora sprang up and ran upstairs. Holly answered the door.

"This is Jason Deere," she announced.

My tall, dark-haired date was extremely good-looking and knew how to make an entrance, stopping a few feet inside the room, smiling at me.

"Okay, let's not make like a *deer* caught in headlights," Frank said. "Line up next to this pretty girl so I can snap a picture and we all can move on."

Jason liked to have his picture taken. He also liked to look at my chest. I wished he'd stop.

"How come you're not covering up for *him?*" Nick whispered as we left the house.

"Excuse me?"

"You know what I'm talking about."

I folded my arms over my chest, but had to unfold them again to walk—it was too difficult to balance with the slim dress and spike heels.

Nick threw back his head and laughed. Both Holly and I glared at him. Jason looked a little mystified but had too much self-confidence to worry about what was going on. He took my hand and drew it lightly through his arm, escorting me to his car.

We arrived at the Queen Victoria just as Jason's ex-girlfriend and her date entered the hotel. Though it was about to pour, we had to wait in the car several minutes to make sure they were settled inside and could watch us arrive. When we finally got to the famous arch of roses, guys gave me the once-over. Girls whispered. Jason's ex checked me out and looked annoyed. Jason was very pleased with this and told me so. I should have realized then what kind of night it was going to be.

Wherever she was, we were, on the carved wood staircase, by the punch-and-cookie tables, near a screen of potted palms. Jason gazed deep in my eyes as if we were madly in love and told boring basketball stories. For the first hour my only real entertainment was watching two girls dump glasses of punch on Nick.

Karen, my guide from earlier in the day, was standing nearby and explained what I had already figured out. "Nick said yes to both of them when they asked him to the prom."

A half hour later he had danced with both of them, and a lot of other girls as well, while Holly directed Steve in his picture taking.

Occasionally Jason would wander off with one of his basketball buddies. Nick had at least two chances to ask me to dance, but didn't.

My feelings aren't hurt, I told myself. But they were.

I tried mixing in with the other kids, asking about their plans for the summer and college, but it was only natural at this last school-sponsored event that they would want to talk about their memories, rather than get to know an outsider. At a band break, while Jason and his buddies recalled another story in the series of their team's greatest moments, I slipped away. I found a velvet love seat, conveniently secluded by palms that separated it from the other chairs. I sank down on it, glad to give my feet and party face a rest.

The fan of palms split. Nick's smile appeared. "Having a good time?" he asked.

"Terrific," I lied.

"How do you like Jason?"

"He's a lot of fun."

"Yeah, I can tell. He's over there, you're here."

"My feet are tired," I explained.

Nick leaned forward, so his face came around the side of the big plant. "That's one of those things I've never understood, girls and shoes. Why are you wearing those instruments of torture?"

I shrugged. "They're Aunt Jule's. They match the dress."

"You could drive their heels through the heart of a vampire."

I laughed and he laughed with me, but his eyes were watchful.

"Sometimes you look so serious," he said.

I glanced away. "Some things in life are serious."

"Ignore them," Nick told me. "I always do."

I met his gaze. "You've been lucky in your life. So far you haven't confronted anything that you can't ignore."

His face grew thoughtful, his eyes a different shade of green. I knew I was looking at him too long. I wished he would take my hand and be as gentle with me as he had been with Nora.

"Jason's looking for you." Holly's voice cut between us.

I straightened up as if our school's headmistress had just walked in.

"For me?" Nick asked mischievously.

"For Lauren."

"Right," I said, standing up.

Holly's voice became warmer. "He's thrilled with you, Lauren. He says he's got the hottest girl at the prom."

"Great." I headed toward Jason without glancing back at her and Nick.

Jason lifted his arm and put it around me as if we had been a couple forever, then went right on talking. I noticed a man wearing rose-tinted glasses standing at the rim of the group of athletes, smiling and nodding. He looked like one of those teachers who wanted to be in with the kids, the kind who went by his first name and didn't realize he was hopelessly uncool.

But I had no one else to talk to. When he followed the cheese tray around the circle to me, I smiled at him.

"I'm Dr. Parker," he said, holding out his hand. "Call me Jim."

"Lauren Brandt," I replied, shaking his hand.

He repeated my name slowly. "Now, how would I know you?"

Judging by his wide, flowered tie, sandals and socks, and the ecology button pinned cockeyed on his shirt, he wasn't a supporter of my father. "I'm staying with my godmother, Jule Ingram, and her daughters, Holly and Nora."

"Oh, yes. Holly and Nora. Two very different girls."

"Have you taught Nora?" I asked eagerly. A teacher's view of her might be helpful.

"No. I'm the school guidance counselor. "

"So you have a background in psychology," I said.

"That's right."

I steered him away from the group. "I have some questions."

"But I have no answers," he replied, smiling.

"My questions are about Nora, not myself," I explained, when we were a distance from the others. "I've known her all my life and I'm really worried. Do you have any idea what's wrong with her?"

Dr. Parker leaned back against a dark wood pillar, crossing one foot over the other, tilting his head at me. I had a feeling he had seen that pose in a movie. "Are you asking for a diagnosis?"

"Well, yes."

"I can't give one without a thorough evaluation," he said.

"But you must have seen her behavior at school," I persisted.

"Yes. And several of her teachers recommended an

evaluation. But her mother would not agree to it. And though I invited Nora to my office a number of times, she never came."

"I can fill you in," I told him. "She's totally phobic about water. My mother drowned here, and Nora says she is sleeping in an old boathouse on the property. She thinks that when the water gets stirred up my mother is doing it. She says my mother is looking for me. Wouldn't you call that crazy?"

He shook his head. "Lauren, it's like asking me if I'd call a painting good, telling me it is blue and red, but not letting me study it firsthand. The answer depends on how those colors are used."

"But my godmother *still* won't agree to an evaluation. And Nora is too confused to know she needs help."

He spread his hands. "Then there's nothing I can do. In my field, if the individual doesn't want help and the person legally responsible refuses to take action, no one else can, not until something life-threatening happens. But I'm glad to talk with *you* about your feelings toward your godmother and Nora."

"I don't want to talk about me!"

He nodded—a little smugly, I thought. "I didn't think so. But just in case you change your mind, here's my card with my summer address and phone. I won't be around school much longer."

I took it from him and read the purple print: *Dr. James Michael Parker, Paranormal Investigator.*

He laughed when he saw the expression on my face. "It's my hobby," he said. "But if you like, I can set you up with a therapist who's more of a straight arrow. Tuck it away in case you need the number."

I thanked him, perhaps not as nicely as I should have, and put it in my purse.

The music had started up again. Jason was in the mood to dance and—what a surprise—found space on the floor next to his ex and her date. Even luckier for me, Nick and Holly were close by.

I knew we were headed for trouble when the slow dance began, but with Nick right there, I had too much pride to duck out to the ladies' room. As we danced, Jason kept moving his head. I figured I was supposed to move mine until our lips would just happen to come within an inch of each other's. I kept my cheek firmly Jason's lapel, figuring the angle would make it harder for him to kiss me.

Meanwhile Holly had her head on Nick's shoulder, her eyes closed. I wondered what it would be like to stand that close to Nick, to feel his arms wrap around me and have him whisper something for my ears alone. I wondered what it would be like to kiss him.

I came back to reality just in time to see Jason's ex kiss her date. Not wanting to be outdone, Jason quickly pulled my face up to his and put his mouth firmly on mine. I turned away.

"Not now," I said, then wanted to kick myself for leaving it open for a later time. But I didn't expect him to interpret my statement as thirty seconds later.

He tried kissing me again.

"No," I said.

He persisted, his hands on the move.

I didn't want to make a scene and embarrass us both. "No," I said quietly, pulling back, "I don't want to make out."

He looked at me, incredulous, then tried again. I pushed him back with both hands. The couples around us started to watch. Holly and Nick stopped dancing.

"What's wrong with you?" Jason said. "Are you frigid? Been going to an all-girl school for too long?"

Now I was furious.

He reached for my arm, trying to pull me back into a close dance. I remembered what Nick had said about Aunt Jule's shoes and vampires. I stepped on Jason's foot, and not with my tippy toes.

Jason yelped and went flying backward. Unfortunately, the punch table was right behind him. It tipped, the huge bowl sliding off, thumping on the carpet, sending up a volcano of pink liquid. Plastic cups tumbled around his head. Nick hooted with laughter.

Humiliated, I hiked up my skirt and ran. I didn't notice the rain till I was halfway down the block from the Queen Victoria, my head swimming with what I imagined others were saying about me. I could hear Nick laughing his sides out. I was sure Holly wasn't happy after all she had done for me. When I'd left, Steve was eagerly snapping pictures that weren't on the approved list.

I held my skirt higher so I could take longer steps and strode for home. An old brown car cruised up beside me.

"Hey, there," Nick said, rolling down the window. "Nice night for a walk."

"Yup."

"Hope that dress doesn't shrink too much. Looks like it's getting shorter."

I silently marched on.

"Maybe you'd like a ride home," Nick suggested.

"I can get there myself."

"I know you can. I was being a gentleman, trying to save the reputation of the guys from Wisteria High."

"I don't judge a whole group by one person."

"Lauren, come on, get in. Like it or not, I'm going to follow you and make sure you get home safely. It will be a lot more comfortable if both of us are riding."

My dress felt like a soaked wool stocking. My hair was hanging in short wet strings, and I figured that my mascara was making black rivers down my cheeks. I had never been more miserable.

Nick got out of the car and ran around to the other side, standing in the pouring rain, gallantly holding the door open. I followed him and got in. By the time he was back in the driver's seat, he was thoroughly wet. His hair looked like it did when we used to swim together, turning into dark gold corkscrews, but his face was very different from the mischievous cherub I once knew. It was chiseled, the jaw line strong, the mouth sensitive—

I quickly looked down and buckled my seat belt. I had seen enough of mouths tonight. It was bewildering to me how much I wanted to avoid Jason's and *didn't* want to avoid Nick's.

"All set?" he asked.

"Yes, thanks." My voice shook a little. I hated it when this happened to me. I could get through all kinds of anger and frustration, but when a crisis was over, I wanted to cry like a baby. I blinked my eyes hard.

"Okay," Nick said. "I'll explain your job. See this string?"

I looked up. It ran from one side of the car to the other, disappearing out the side windows. Peering through the fogged windshield, I realized the string made a big loop and was tied to the wipers.

"The blades don't work," Nick said. "So you have to grab hold of this string and pull. Left, right, left, right. Got it?"

I looked at him for a moment, then moved the string to the left. In unison, the wipers moved to the right.

"You're going to have to do it faster than that," he said.

I started smiling. "This is crazy."

"Left, right, faster, faster—there you go."

"Why don't you get them fixed?" I asked.

"It's more fun this way."

"I hope you don't feel the same about brakes. They don't need fixing, do they?"

"Why do you think I wear these thick rubber soles?"

I laughed. "You're kidding."

"You can try dragging your foot," he continued, "but I don't think those heels will do much more than knock off menacing forms of life."

I laughed again. "They are pretty good at that."

I liked being in the old car with Nick. I liked there

being nothing but rain and us. He turned on the radio, which had lousy reception. I didn't care. I could have ridden around with him for hours. Probably all his other one-night girls had felt the same way.

Nick pulled up to the edge of Aunt Jule's driveway. "Last time I went down there in the rain, I had to be towed out," he said.

"No problem. Thanks for the ride."

"I'll walk you to the door."

"No, you'll get wetter than you already are," I told him, "then drip all over the dance floor."

Nick reached over the seat. "I just happen to have a shower curtain with me."

"You do? Why?"

"It's showering," he said, then pulled it over his head and got out of the car. I watched him hop over the puddles to my side.

"I use it as a drop cloth when I'm painting at Frank's," he explained as he opened my door and helped me out. Still holding my hand, he used his other to grab an edge of the curtain. I did the same and we made our way down the driveway.

My slim skirt made it difficult. I needed a third hand to hold up my dress. Suddenly I lurched forward. My heels had stuck firmly in the mud, pitching me headlong.

"Whoa!" Nick cried, dropping his part of the shower curtain, catching me around the waist. He straightened me up like a toppled-over mannequin, trying to get me back in my shoes.

I felt my way with my toes and was standing

squarely again, but Nick didn't let go. The shower curtain rested on our heads like a collapsed tent. He
ignored it, facing me now, his arms around me, his eyes
shining softly. My hands rested on his shoulders.

"Hi," he said.

"Hi."

"I'd like to kiss you." He waited a moment for my
response, then added, "Or, if you'd rather, we can
dance, as long as we can get you unstuck."

"I think I'm in deep."

"Me, too," he said, looking into my eyes.

His head moved closer to mine. Then he lifted his
hand, cupping my cheek ever so gently. His lips touched
my lips, light as a butterfly, once, twice.

The kisses were lovely, so lovely I couldn't help it—I
did a totally stupid, uncool thing. I sighed.

I heard the laughter rumbling inside Nick and I
started to pull away. But his arms wrapped around me.
He held me close and pressed his lips against mine. A
thrill went through me. I kissed him back—I didn't
think about it, just kissed him with all that my heart
felt.

Now Nick pulled back, looking at me surprised. I
wondered if I had done something wrong. My only
experience was a smattering of hardly-touch good-night
kisses after dance dates. What if I had done something
weird and didn't know it?

"I—I have to go," I said, ducking out from under the
shower curtain, making a dash for the porch without
my shoes.

When I glanced back Nick was wearing the curtain

like a cape, watching me run to the house. He turned away slowly and walked back to his car.

I stood inside the door and ran one muddy foot over the other. Aunt Jule's red shoes were stuck in the driveway, like little memorials at the magical place where Nick and I had kissed.

ten

Aunt Jule looked up from her book, silent for a moment, surveying me. "Oh, dear."

"I hope I haven't embarrassed Holly," I said, entering the river room.

"What happened? Where's Jason?"

"I left him on the dance floor, sprawled on it."

She laughed and pointed to the chair next to her. "Sit. Tell."

I did. When I had finished, Aunt Jule smiled. "And you seem so sweet and innocent. I bet he was surprised."

Not as surprised as Nick, I thought, recalling the expression on his face a few minutes before. I decided not to tell Aunt Jule that Nick had brought me home. She'd want every detail.

After cleaning the mud from my feet and wiping up the tracks I'd left in the hall, I headed upstairs, reliving in my mind Nick's wonderful kiss. On the landing I stopped abruptly. Nora stood near the top of the stairway, as if waiting for me. Her hand gripped the banister, her fine bones exaggerated by the tension in her. The light shining from below threw Nora's tall shadow against the wall, trapping it within the bars cast by the railing.

"Is everything okay?" I asked.

Her voice shook: "Someone doesn't like it when you wear that dress. Someone doesn't like it when you wear that heart."

"I'm taking off the dress," I told her, "but not the heart."

"Someone will be very angry."

"Do you mean my mother?" I wondered if "Sondra's" feelings were actually a projection of Nora's.

"I won't tell," she whispered.

"Won't tell what?" I asked loudly, and she drew back as if I'd threatened her.

"Don't tell!" she exclaimed. "Don't even think the words!" She lifted her hands and held the sides of her head. "Thinking can make it happen," she moaned, then hurried down the steps.

I stared after her, trying to understand the darkness inside her. I'd lock my door again tonight.

Aunt Jule had laughed about the shoes stuck in the driveway and told me to leave them and trash them tomorrow. I had dumped my muddy stockings in the bedroom wastebasket and hung up the dress to dry. A long hot shower had washed away the last bits of mud and mascara, but not my apprehensiveness toward Nora.

I had to admit to myself that I wasn't simply afraid *for* her but *of* her. The fact that Aunt Jule and Nick saw nothing in her to fear, and even Holly didn't think her sister would harm others, made me feel alone. I worried that my own mind was playing tricks on me—perhaps I had never heard a voice like my mother's.

I tried to read myself to sleep, but it was useless. When the bedroom lights of Aunt Jule and Nora finally went off, I pulled on shorts beneath my nightshirt and went downstairs again. On the garden side of the house, I restlessly walked the porch.

My thoughts shifted to Nick. I couldn't believe I had kissed him, not just with my lips but my heart. Until now, it had been easy to blame my mother for her screwed-up life, labeling her as one of those girls who couldn't live without a guy, who set herself up for disaster. But here I was, falling fast.

And what about Holly? I had told myself that she wasn't really drawn to Nick—she wasn't hooked on him. But by nature Holly was cool and collected, so there was no way to tell. It didn't matter. Nick had clearly explained his dating policy: one girl after the next. After the prom he'd be working on whoever stood in line behind Holly and me. The red shoes seemed symbolic—abandoned in the mud.

I gazed out in their direction. The rain had stopped and the moon was peeking through quick-moving clouds, splashing silver on the soaked gardens and long path. What if Holly came home with Nick, found the shoes, and dumped them in the trash?

I had to have them.

I trudged through the mud, feeling foolish. The ruined shoes were useless—all I could do was display them next to my softball trophies. But I *had* to have them.

When I returned to the house, my feet looked as if I'd put on brown moccasins. I set down the high heels and headed for the greenhouse to fetch a bucket of water for dipping. I was just beyond the knot garden when I thought I heard a door open on the upper porch. Turning toward the house, I surveyed it.

"Hello," I called softly.

No one answered, but I saw the slight movement in the shadows. If it were Aunt Jule, she would have replied. It had to be Nora, I thought, and continued on, determined not to be cowed by her.

The air was still and heavy, as water-saturated as the ground. It was the kind of humid Shore night I remembered as a child, when a light left on became a halo of mist and insects. When I entered the greenhouse, I kept the lights off so I wouldn't be swarmed.

In the intermittent moonlight the glass house looked surreal. Plants, looming tall in the darkness, suddenly caught the light and seemed to bristle and straighten as I came near. Spider plants drooped long tongues over the edges of hanging pots. Short, thick plants reached out, then curled back on themselves with crooked stems.

Moonlit raindrops and condensation kept me from seeing beyond the glass panes. As I moved among rows of plants, I couldn't get over the feeling that someone was outside watching me.

Something brushed my arm and I jumped. Just a

branch, Lauren, I chided myself. Watch where you're going and stop imagining things.

Still, the skin on my arms prickled as I moved toward the back of the greenhouse searching for a bucket. There was something in here with me—I could feel it—some disturbance in the air. There was no rational way to explain the sensation; the air didn't move, but something unseen moved through it. I walked in the center of the main aisle and kept my arms close against my sides, reluctant to touch any of the plants.

Along the back wall was a bucket and six pots of vines, young plants that Nora was training on two-foot trellises. I leaned over to pick up the bucket. Something rustled. I glanced left, then right, and told myself I was acting paranoid.

I heard it again, soft but distinct, like leaves tussling in a breeze, though the air was as motionless as before. My forehead felt damp. A trickle of sweat ran down my neck.

I quickly picked up the bucket, then noticed the twisted shape of the vine growing next to it. The vine wasn't just twined around the trellis, but knotted to it, its delicate tendrils tied in minuscule knots. I shivered, and with my free hand touched my necklace, running my finger along its smooth chain. Last night it had borne the same kind of knots. I looked at the other young vines. They were all knotted, some of their roots pulled up as if the force used to tie them had yanked them from the soil.

Clutching the steel handle of the bucket, I walked

quickly toward the greenhouse sink, wanting to get the water and get out of there. But when I reached for the faucet, I stopped. On the shelf above the sink sat a jade plant, its fleshy almond-shaped leaves glimmering in the moonlight. It moved. I took a step back, staring at it, knowing it was impossible, but certain I had seen it. The branches had moved, as if invisible fingers had riffled them.

I was going crazy. I was seeing what my mother had seen before she died, things knotting, things moving. *"There's no hand touching them, baby. They move by themselves."* Maybe Aunt Jule was right: I was obsessed with my mother, so much so that I was imagining her experiences.

I fought the panic rising in me and reached for the faucet again, turning the handle hard. When the bucket was half full, I shut off the stream.

I thought I felt a trickle on my neck—spray from the faucet or my own sweat. Reaching up to wipe it, I touched dry skin and my necklace. It wasn't water, but the chain creeping along my neck. I looked down at the silver heart, rising like a slow tide, moving closer and closer to my throat. I dropped the bucket and spun around, as if to catch someone pulling the necklace, but no one was there. I clawed at the chain, grabbing it before it could choke me, and yanked down. It snapped. Holding it tightly in my fist, I ran.

When I was outside the greenhouse, nearly at the porch, I opened my fingers and gazed down at the chain. The end of it was tied in a tiny knot.

eleven

I slept little that night. Whenever I did drift off, I slipped into dreams of swimming through dark water with rope-like plants winding around my arms and legs. The next morning, when I was fully awake, I thought I might have dreamed the events in the greenhouse. Then I found my chain on the bureau, broken and knotted at one end.

I had no idea how to account for what I had experienced last night. I didn't want to think that Nora's distorted perception of the world was infecting me, making me see things that weren't real. But I had never believed in ghosts or other paranormal phenomena. It was terrifying to think that a power I didn't understand was present when Nora was. How could I defend myself against something I couldn't see?

When I got down to the kitchen, Holly was sitting at the table writing up another of her lists, looking chipper as usual despite her late night. Her steadiness had a calming effect on me. I poured a glass of juice and sat down across from her.

"Listen, Holly, I'm sorry if I embarrassed you last night when—"

She held up a hand. "Hey, cut it out. We both know Jason was acting like a jerk. He asked for it and you gave it to him."

I relaxed. "I wasn't sure you'd see it that way."

"Are you kidding? I wish I had a couple girlfriends like you. You're sweet to a point," she said, smiling, "but then you deliver the news straight."

I was surprised and pleased.

"By the way, I put your purse on the hall table. You left it at the Queen."

"Thanks. I forgot all about it." I took a long drink of juice. "So what can I do for the party? Clean? Pick up groceries?"

"I'd love it if you'd get the party platters from Dee's. They'll be ready at two."

"Okay. How about before that?"

"Well, since you've offered," she said, "there's about a million things."

We were going over the list when Nick showed up with Rocky. I felt suddenly guilty. Holly might not wish she had girlfriends like me if she knew that I had kissed her prom date. But Nick gave no sign of anything special having happened between him and me. In fact, I got a much warmer greeting from Rocky—a joyful bark, several head butts, and a lot of tail-wagging.

"Are you giving him treats on the sly?" Nick asked me.

"No. I guess I just smell right to him."

"Like waterfowl?" Nick replied, laughing. "That's his favorite scent."

I noticed that Nick didn't behave in any special way toward Holly, either, which seemed to confirm my theory that at tonight's party she and I would watch him move on to the next girl—if there was one in the senior class whom he still hadn't dated.

Nora walked in while Nick and Holly were discussing what they needed to borrow from Frank.

"Hey, Nora," he said softly.

"Hey, Nick."

"Hi, Nora," I greeted her.

She didn't respond.

Holly said nothing to her sister. Perhaps she was used to Nora's cold treatment and didn't try anymore.

"Nora, was that you on the porch late last night?" I asked.

She turned to me as if she had finally realized I was there. "I don't remember."

"Try to," I said firmly.

Nick and Holly glanced at me.

"It was someone else," Nora replied. "Someone else did it."

"Did what?" Holly asked.

"Don't tell," Nora said, fingering the collar of her shirt.

Holly gazed at me expectantly.

"Nothing really," I replied. "I was out walking and went in the greenhouse. I thought I heard something stirring in there."

"Like an animal?" Holly asked.

"I don't know what it was. I was curious if Nora saw or heard anything."

Nora turned her back on us and rummaged through the kitchen cabinets. Holly pressed her lips together, looking as if she didn't completely believe my story. She'd believe me even less if I told her that a plant moved on its own and my necklace tried to choke me. I needed to talk to someone about what was happening, but not someone practical like her, or emotional and defensive like Aunt Jule. I wasn't ready to turn my mind over to the psychologist in the pink glasses. Still, it scared me to be alone with Nora in these strange experiences that were somehow connected to my mother's death. I needed to talk to Nick.

My chance came about an hour later, when I had stopped hosing off lawn chairs to play with Rocky. After several retrievals of his soggy ball, Nick's dog was trying to con me into the water, not bringing the ball to my hand, but releasing it a few feet offshore. The river was plenty warm for swimming, but I still didn't want to wade in it. And I still hadn't walked to the end of the dock.

"He wants you to swim with him," Nick said, coming up behind me.

I turned. "So I can doggy paddle around with that disgusting ball in my mouth? I don't think so."

Nick grinned.

I glanced past him, surveying the lawn and porches. No one was in sight. "Nick, I need to talk to you."

I saw him tense.

"About Nora," I added quickly, afraid he'd think I was bringing up the kiss.

"Okay," he said after a moment of hesitation. "What's up?"

"I know you believe that Nora wouldn't hurt a fly," I began, "but some strange things have been happening and I'm getting scared."

"Scared of what?" he asked.

"Nora is obsessed with my mother's death. You heard her last night, talking as if my mother could come back from the dead."

He nodded.

"She thinks my mother is looking for me, that my mother stirs up the water in the boathouse, that she gets angry because I'm wearing Aunt Jule's necklace and dress."

Rocky raced over and dropped the ball at our feet. When neither of us picked it up, he ran off with it again.

"Nora is haunted by her," I went on. "It's as if guilt has kept my mother alive in Nora's mind."

Nick pulled back from me. "Wait a minute. You're not suggesting that—"

I rushed on: "What if my mother's death wasn't an accident?"

"The police said it was."

"But Aunt Jule stopped them before they investigated."

He shook his head. "No. You're way off base. Nora is neurotic and confused, but she's not capable of murdering someone."

"How do you know that?" I asked.

"It's just not in her to harm others."

"Nick, there are things inside of Nora that none of us understand."

"Like what?" he challenged me.

"Voices, for one thing. Even as a child she answered questions no one asked her—you must remember that. There are things she sees and hears that we don't."

I didn't add that I feared those things had a reality beyond the one we grasped and that I was starting to have experiences as strange as hers. His quickness to defend Nora had cooled my trust in his ability to keep an open mind.

"Lauren," he said, "I know how hard it must be for you coming back here. The memories are terrible. I've noticed how you look away from the dock and don't want to go into the water. You are haunted, too."

"Yes, but—"

He rested a hand on my arm. "Hear me out. I understand why you'd want to blame another person for your mother's death. When we lose someone we love very much, we want reasons."

"Don't patronize me," I said, shaking off his hand.

"I'm not. It's just that I've seen this before. Years ago, the Christmas Frank's wife died in a car accident, her family couldn't accept it. They accused Frank, saying he was after her money and property. Aunt Margaret's death was painful enough for him without their making him a murder suspect. But I understand their reaction. Fate and chance—they don't seem enough to explain terrible losses. We all want someone to point to and be angry at."

I pressed my lips together.

"Even so, you can't go around blaming innocent people. Nora is very fragile. Be gentle with her. Don't do anything to make things harder for her."

It seemed to me that Nora was doing plenty to make things harder for me.

"Now hear *me* out," I replied. "Yesterday I went to see my mother's grave in the churchyard across from your school. There is another grave next to it. Its stone is inscribed with the word *Daughter*."

Nick blinked but said nothing.

"When I got back to my car, I found a note that someone had slipped through the front window, a plain piece of paper with two words: *You're next*."

"When did you go there?" he asked.

"Right after I left the school. Nick, I know that Holly thinks Nora never leaves home, but she does. She was shadowing me at the festival Sunday."

"That proves nothing," he said, "especially since what you just described is a prank that could be played on anyone walking through a cemetery. It happened after school let out. Someone hanging around saw you enter the place—they didn't know you—they just thought it'd be fun to leave the note and get a reaction," he reasoned. "It was nothing but a joke. You're reading into it."

"If the person didn't know me, how would he or she know which car was mine?"

"This is a small town. Everyone knows the visitors from the residents. You have a D.C. tag, don't you?"

"Yes."

"There you go. Did you happen to stop at your car between the school and cemetery?"

I nodded, remembering that I had put my purse in the trunk.

"Mystery solved."

"No," I told him, "there's something more going on, and I'm going to find out what it is."

He shook his head. "You're going to make yourself as miserable and crazy as Nora. Your mother is gone, Lauren. I know this sounds harsh, but you have to get over it." He turned away from me and whistled for Rocky.

I have to get over *him,* I thought, as the two of us walked off in opposite directions.

I was glad to get away from the house that afternoon. I picked up the party platters at two and paid for them, making them an extra graduation gift to Holly. She was probably hoping I'd do that, but I didn't mind.

Dee's was on the other side of Oyster Creek, outside of town. On the way home I passed the small road that led to Nick's house and started thinking about the way he protected Nora. I was glad I hadn't mentioned the knots to him, for he wouldn't have believed me. Why give him more reasons to claim that I was going to make myself as miserable and crazy as Nora?

A loud *crack* shattered my thoughts. I quickly veered to the right, not seeing what had struck my car, instinctively getting out of the way. My car flew over the edge of the road. The wheel jerked in my hands and I struggled to control it. I hit something, hit it hard, and heard the sound of metal bending and scraping. For a fraction of a second my body was thrown forward, then the airbag buffeted me back.

I sat there stunned, staring at the windshield, a spider web of cracked glass with a large chip at the center. After a few moments I unbuckled my seat belt, opened the door, and climbed out shakily.

My Honda had become wedged between two trees, entangled in barbed wire fencing. I leaned against the side of it, too limp to get my cell phone from my purse.

A car passed by, then its brake lights flashed on and the driver backed up.

"Lauren!" Frank said, pulling himself out of his tiny sports car. "What happened?"

"I'm not sure."

He quickly strode toward me.

"As I was coming around the bend, something hit my windshield. I shied away from it and ended up here."

"Something like what?" Frank asked. "A stone, a bird, fruit off a truck?"

"I didn't see."

Frank walked around to the front of my car surveying it with a grim face and sharp eyes. He examined the windshield, then whistled softly. "I don't like telling you this, Lauren, but that was no pebble that ricocheted against your windshield. It was something heavy and I suspect it was thrown."

twelve

I gazed at the big chip in the glass and the splintered lines radiating from it. "I figured something had been hurled at me."

"Did you now?" he replied, studying me curiously. "Did you see someone by the side of the road?"

"No, but I was on automatic pilot," I admitted, "thinking about a lot of stuff." I retrieved my purse from the car floor. "I'd better call the police to report this and find out whose fence I've ruined."

Frank slipped his own phone from his pocket. "Don't bother," he said. "The sheriff's a busybody. I can track down the owner and help you if your insurance doesn't cover the damages. Who do you want to tow your car? Pete? He still has the Crown station on Jib Street."

"That's fine."

While Frank made the call I examined the front of my car. By sheer luck it had run between two trees, plowing into the fence. The trees were planted in even intervals along the stretch of road, about a car width apart. If I had steered a little to the left or right, I would have hit a tree head on. Before braking I had been going the standard speed for country roads, 50 mph. The accident could have been a lot more serious.

Frank clicked off his phone. "Someone will be here in about fifteen minutes. Let's see if we can find what hit you."

It wasn't hard. Rocks don't abound on the Eastern Shore, and bricks aren't part of the natural landscape. The only thing on the road and its sandy shoulder was a half a brick. Frank picked it up and showed it to me, his face thoughtful, then placed it on my car's hood.

We transferred the party food to his car. Fortunately the cold cuts and bread had not been made into sandwiches and could be rearranged at home. We had just finished when a sheriff's car put on its flashers and pulled over. A small man with a round, sunburned face climbed out and ambled toward us.

"Frank," he said, nodding his head.

"Tom," Frank replied coolly, his tone indicating that this was the man he didn't like.

The sheriff introduced himself simply as "McManus."

"Now let's see," he said, "Blue Honda, D.C. tag. I don't have any report of this, and I just checked in."

"It just happened," Frank replied.

The sheriff asked to see my license and began to question me. It was routine stuff, but the last question caught me by surprise: "Is there anyone you're not getting along with these days?"

"Uh, no," I told him, "not really."

"And who would be in your not-really category?"

Nora, Jason. "No one," I said.

He studied me for a moment. I gazed back at him as steadily as possible.

"Kids," McManus said at last. "One day after school's out and they don't know what to do with themselves. I'm sorry about this, Miss Brandt. It doesn't make our town look good."

"It can happen anywhere," I replied.

"Hope your insurance covers most of it. Well, here comes Pete's boy." The sheriff gestured toward the tow truck as he walked back to his car.

Pete's "boy" looked about thirty and seemed pleased to be towing my Honda. "She's real pretty," he said, "even with barbed wire wrapped around her."

Frank winked at me, then helped the mechanic disentangle the car. I filled out a form and was told to check in with Pete after talking to my insurance company.

When Frank and I finally headed home in his car, I thanked him for helping me out.

"No problem," he said. "That's what neighbors are for." We rumbled over the creek bridge. "So, how's Nora?"

I could guess why he was asking. "She's not that good at softball, Frank."

He laughed. "Well put. I didn't think she had that kind of aim. Of course, she could get lucky." Then his face grew serious. "Does she have any friends nowadays? Could she have gotten someone else to throw the brick for her?"

"As far as I know she doesn't trust anyone but Holly and Nick."

"Are there any other candidates for Wisteria's Hoodlum of the Year? I know the sheriff already asked, but it didn't sound like you were saying anything more than you had to."

"I had nothing concrete to tell him," I explained. "It's possible my date for the prom decided to get back at me. I kind of landed him on the floor with the punch bowl."

"So I heard," Frank said, grinning. "Of course, Jason would have a good throwing arm," he pointed out.

I nodded, unconvinced Jason had done it.

We were silent the last few blocks home, then Frank suddenly swore and swerved, narrowly avoiding the deep mud of Aunt Jule's driveway. "You need a sled around here," he said as he parked the car on the street. "Why doesn't she pave the thing? Oh, I know. She can't afford it."

As we got out to unload the food Aunt Jule emerged from the house.

"Jule, come here a sec," Frank hollered.

I could tell from the stiffness in her back that she didn't like being summoned by him. Before she said something unfriendly, I interjected, "I had an accident, Aunt Jule, and Frank stopped to help me."

She hurried down the path in her bare feet, not caring about the mud. "Are you all right? What kind of accident?"

I explained what happened.

"It was a near miss," Frank told her.

My godmother reached for me and hugged me tightly .

"Jule," Frank said, "is there anyone you know out to get Lauren?"

She let go of me abruptly. "What a ridiculous thing to ask!"

"Maybe, maybe not," he replied. "The last time Lauren was here her mother met with a fatal accident. At least we called it an accident. The sheriff isn't calling this one anything other than deliberate. The only question is whether it was random or not."

Aunt Jule's eyes flashed. "No one who knows Lauren would want to hurt her. And I resent what you're implying about Sondra's death. It was an accident—just like Margaret's," she added slyly.

I figured the reference to his wife was meant to sting, but Frank responded mildly. "I guess that's why it's got me concerned. This was awfully similar to Marge's accident, and she was killed instantly."

The color drained from Aunt Jule's face.

The porch door banged back, and Holly stepped outside. "Hey, Lauren, did you get everything?"

"Yes, I'll bring it in."

"Nick, we need help," I heard Holly say. He followed her out of the house and down the path. "Where's your car?" Holly asked, when she and Nick reached us.

Frank filled them in on the accident. Aunt Jule listened to the details for a second time, rubbing one hand over the other. Holly grilled me with more questions.

"I can't believe it!" she exclaimed at the end. "People are such jerks!"

Nick stood next to her silently, a wary expression on his face. Perhaps he was waiting for me to blame Nora. But even if I were positive that Nora was behind this, I wouldn't have accused her. The more I tried to convince Aunt Jule and him that something was seriously wrong, the more they denied it.

"Well, let's get the food into the fridge," I said. "Thanks for stopping, Frank. I was pretty rattled."

"No problem," he replied. "Call me if you need anything."

I needed a clone—a look-alike who would go to the party, swim in the dark river, and act cool around Nick. It was nearly six o'clock and I still hadn't put on my bathing suit.

Holly stopped by my room to warn me that the entire class was invited, so Jason would be coming.

"I figured that."

"Do you need a suit?" she asked, noticing my shorts and shirt. Then she grinned. "Do we dare to see what Mom has in her closet? Maybe a crochet bikini with matching beach mules?"

I laughed out loud. "Think I'll pass on that."

"You know, I'm glad to have your help tonight, Lauren. Really, I'm desperate for it! But you're going to party, too, right?"

"Right," I replied, planning to keep a low profile.

It wasn't hard at a gathering attended by eighty kids. Jason, his buddies, and several girls passed by without noticing me while I was setting out trays of food. Rocky found me, but Nick was nowhere in sight. Frank came over about eight-thirty to munch and admire the work we'd done. He had lent Holly two dozen torches, which made a fiery trail down to the river. His strings of outdoor lights and electric generator had the dock glowing like Christmas.

"Doesn't it look terrific?" I asked.

"Yup! It's a perfect site for a party," he said, surveying the landscape. "Where's Jule?"

"Last time I saw her, on the upper porch."

"Great chaperon," he observed.

"Don't worry," I teased, "if there's any trouble I'll come get you."

"Will you?" he replied, grinning. "I'm locking the door and pulling the shades. I guess Nora doesn't show up for these things."

"She's probably hiding in her room."

Frank asked about the estimate Pete had given me on my car. "Not too bad," he said. "Not nearly as bad as I thought it'd be, but if your insurance company gives you any grief, let me know. I'll tell them what they need to hear." He moved on, then stopped twenty feet away to survey the partyscape again and smile at someone. I followed his gaze to Nick.

I thought I had caught Nick's eye, but he turned away and I didn't see him for another hour. Holly and I were kneeling on the ground, bent over bags of ice, trying to break apart the cubes.

"Muscles, just in time!" Holly said, smiling up at him.

He didn't smile back—barely acknowledged her—fixing his gaze on me. In the flickering torchlight he looked different, his jaw set, his eyes intense.

"I want to talk to you, Lauren."

I saw Holly raise an eyebrow. "Shall I leave?" she asked, a note of irritation in her voice.

"No," he replied quickly. "This isn't private. I want to thank you, Lauren, for getting my cartoon pulled from the newspaper."

"What?"

"The cartoon you saw hanging above my drafting table, the one I sold to the Easton paper."

I looked at Nick confused. "What about it?"

"Aren't they running it?" Holly asked.

"No."

She frowned. "Did they give you a reason why?"

"Oh, yeah, they gave me a reason. Editorial decision. Funny thing, the editors loved it last week."

"I don't understand," I said. "Why did they change their minds?"

He stared at me coldly.

I stood up. "You *can't* be blaming me."

"Who else on the Shore would want to protect your father?" he asked.

"I resent that."

"I resent your getting my cartoon pulled."

"But I didn't!"

Holly rose and stood next to me. "Perhaps, Nick, you should have asked for a more specific reason than *editorial decision.*"

"I did, several times, but they were evasive. Obviously, someone has put pressure on the paper. Maybe not you, Lauren, maybe it was your father or his supporters. But then, how would they know about the cartoon? Who would have seen it and told them?"

I shook my head at him, amazed that he would accuse me.

"Things like small publications may not seem important to you," Nick went on. "You've got connections—people will bend over backward for Senator Brandt's kid. But I have to earn my way. One publication leads to the next. Every acceptance is important to me."

"How can you think I'd do that to you?" I demanded. "I wouldn't do it to anyone! I thought you knew me better."

He glanced past me, then met my eyes with steely intensity. "So did I."

thirteen

Nick strode away. I stood there dumbfounded. When I finally realized Holly's hand was resting on my shoulder, I turned to her.

"Don't worry about it," she said. "When Nick cools down, I'll talk to him."

"I didn't ask them to pull it, Holly."

"I believe you. And after I talk to Nick, he will, too."

"Maybe." I looked down at the lumpy bags of ice, then picked up one of the crab mallets that we were using as hammers. "Leave this job to me. I'll enjoy it."

She laughed. "Go for it, girl."

I banged away, feeling better with each shattering of ice. Several guys tried to help, but I politely declined their offers and filled up two cold chests by myself.

Karen, my guide at the yearbook office, stopped to talk. Redheaded Steve came by and told me he had a photo of Jason and me at the prom, posing inside the arch of roses, and several excellent shots of Jason lying among the punch cups. Steve was hoping Holly would okay his before-and-after idea.

I laughed in spite of myself.

A little while later Holly tried to get me involved in the party by asking me to help with the dancing-on-the-dock contest. We played music while blindfolded couples slow danced, trying not to fall in the water. Jason and a pretty girl went quickly. Nick and his partner didn't tumble over till near the end.

We awarded silly prizes and the party went on. Some kids hung out on the dock, some swam, and others sat in groups scattered over the lawn. I wanted to leave but was afraid I'd hurt Holly's feelings. I sat with Karen and her friends from yearbook, watching the party like a movie, trying hard to keep my eyes off Nick.

"Earth to Lauren," Karen said.

"Sorry, what?"

"We're going up on the dock. Want to come?"

I hesitated. "Okay."

I followed the group, wishing I had made myself walk to the end of the dock before the party. A tall guy, one of Jason's friends, was giving the girls a leg up, but when it was my turn, he withdrew his hand.

"Well, look who it is."

"Hi," I said, and climbed onto the dock unassisted.

Jason's friend leaped up behind me.

"Want to play tag?" he asked. "We're getting up a game of water tag."

"Thanks, but no thanks. I was following Karen."

When I tried to move on, he stepped on my heel. "Don't you swim?"

"I do, but I don't want to tonight."

"Why not tonight?" he persisted.

"I'm not in the mood. And I'm not wearing a bathing suit," I added, walking ahead.

He caught me by the elbow. "You know how to swim better than your mother, right?"

That didn't deserve a response. I strode toward the end of the T-shaped dock and tried to turn right, where Karen had gone. But Jason's friend followed and deftly stepped in front of me, separating me from my group.

"Come on. You can swim in what you're wearing."

"I really don't want to."

"Water's warm." There was no warmth in his voice.

He took a quick step toward me, and I moved away, toward the left side of the dock. Kids lined both sides of the walkway, dangling their feet over the river. As the guy pressed forward, the only thing I could do was continue to the left. We reached the end of that part of the dock.

"Hey, everybody, look who I found," he announced to the kids gathered in the water below us.

I gazed down at the place where my mother had died. For a moment all I could see were the dark river and blurs of swimmers looking up at me, the party lights turning their shiny skins green and orange. The faces of Jason and his teammates slowly came into focus.

"I tried to get her to come in, but she doesn't want to play with us."

"Aw," one guy said mockingly.

"Snob," said another.

"Step on her foot, Ken," Jason suggested.

Ken moved closer to me. Feeling lightheaded, I reached for a piling to steady myself. The wood was wet and I shrank from it. It was the piling on which my mother had bled.

With a sudden move Ken pulled my knees out from under me, flipping me into the water. For a moment I was stunned by the impact and cold. The black river rushed over my head. My ears felt swollen from the surge of water. I hit bottom, kicked hard, and surfaced.

Jason and his friends encircled me. They were tall enough to keep their heads above water, but I had to tread. Jason reached out, his wide hand coming down swiftly on my head, shoving me under. I pushed up, angry, gasping for air. Laughing faces surrounded me.

Another hand hovered, then pushed me down. I fought my way back to the surface and tried to swim away, going left, then right. Their circle tightened. They shoved me under and held me there. When I surfaced, I tried to call for help, but I didn't have enough air in my lungs. They kept pushing me down like a bobbing toy. I began to panic. The taste of river mud was in my mouth. I saw black spots, as if the darkness of the water was seeping into my brain. My stomach cramped and I doubled over.

Then a force came rushing through the water, scattering us. The circle broke. I swam through it and kept swimming, wanting to stop for breath, but not daring to. When I kicked my foot against the bottom I finally stood up, breathing hard, with the water just above my knees. Rocky was next to me.

I heard the raucous laughter behind me. "Dumb dog!"

"Smart dog," I whispered to Rocky as we waded to shore.

Holly and Nick were standing close together at the edge of the water.

"I knew you should have put on a suit," Holly said, smiling at me.

I stared at her. Didn't she realize what those guys were doing? Didn't she see how scared I was?

"They're a mean group," I said.

She frowned. "What do you mean?"

"They knew I was out of breath."

"Oh, Lauren, they were just having fun."

"Then their sense of fun is warped."

She didn't get it—she seemed amused. "The guys were teasing you. It's how they flirt."

I turned to Nick, but he said nothing. I wondered what he would have done if they had "teased" Nora like that. "I'm going in."

"You're coming back, aren't you?" Holly asked.

"No." The dog was still by my side. "Nick, I want to take Rocky with me. I'll let him out later, okay?"

"He's going to smell awful," Holly reminded me.

"Fine," Nick said with a shrug.

When I got to the kitchen, I gave Rocky a bowl of water and a piece of turkey. "Sorry I don't have any waterfowl to offer you." I found an old towel and dried him off as best I could. "I don't know what I would have done without you, big guy," I whispered.

Holding on to his tags so they wouldn't jingle, I led Rocky upstairs. I heard Aunt Jule's television and tip-toed past her bedroom. When I was a child, I told my godmother everything. It hurt not to trust her now, but I could guess what she'd say if I recounted the incident in the river. At best, she'd dismiss it, seeing it as Holly did; at worst, she'd say I was obsessed with my mother's drowning.

Nora's door was closed as usual. So was mine, though I didn't remember shutting it. I opened the door and flicked on the overhead light. Rocky trotted in hap-pily. I stood frozen in the doorway, surveying my room in disbelief.

The curtains hung half off the rod, as if someone had yanked on them furiously, each panel tied in a knot. The sheets were pulled off the bed and twisted grotesquely, their corners in knots. My bedside lamp lay on its side, its shade bent, its cord knotted. My heart necklace, muddy stockings, and the bras in my laundry hamper were all tied in knots. Now I knew how my mother had felt—this attack was personal.

I pulled open bureau drawers. My clothes were a mess, rolled up on themselves as if someone had tried tying their clumsy shapes. In the closet, the arms of my long-sleeved shirts were knotted.

Just touching the knots made me feel creepy, but I had to get rid of them. As I untied my things, I reviewed the events of the last three days, trying to determine what was truly a threat and cause for fear. The water in the boathouse was probably stirred by a wake. The note left in my car and the brick thrown at my windshield could have been done by or for Nora, but they also could have been random pranks. It seemed likely that the harassment in the river was revenge for decking Jason at the prom. Setting aside those events, the strangest ones remained: the swing incident, the nighttime experience in the greenhouse, and these knots.

I thought about showing some of the knots to Holly, then I kept on untying. Like me, Holly saw that Nora had serious problems and she wanted those problems fixed, but the incident with Jason's friends had made it clear—Holly read only the surface of things. I was convinced there was a lot going on beneath it. As for Frank, I didn't see how I could talk to him about things that sounded so crazy.

I had untied everything but my heart necklace. I stared down at its tiny knots, thinking about the way the chain had crept along my neck, the way the jade plant moved on its own, and the swing rope snapped and knotted. What power was at work here? The power of my own imagination and fear—or something stranger—an invisible, dangerous thing?

I pulled out the card with Dr. Parker's number and reached for my cell phone. I was finally scared to the point of desperate. My mother had seen things knotted in the weeks before she died. Now I was.

fourteen

dr. Parker's pink glasses looked like magic spectacles in the lava-lamp interior of Wayne's Bar. When he'd asked me to meet him there at eleven P.M., I'd wondered what I was getting myself into, but Wayne's turned out to be a health bar serving various flavors of springwater, herbal teas, and vegetable dishes, some of which looked suspiciously like cooked bay grass.

I was sipping my raspberry water and staring at Dr. Parker's glasses, as if an answer might suddenly rise to the surface of them the way it does on a Magic 8 Ball. He had listened without interrupting while I recounted some of the events of seven years ago and the strange things that had been happening recently. Now he was either thinking or asleep.

"An interesting image," he murmured, then opened his eyes. "Tell me, Lauren, tell me all about knots. What do they mean?"

I stared at him blankly. "I don't want to be rude, but I thought you were going to explain them."

"If you were writing a poem," he said, "and used a knot as a symbol, an image, what might it stand for?"

I gazed down at my hands, twisting my fingers around one another.

"Think of all the different kinds of knots you have seen," he prompted, "not just the recent ones—others. What do they do? How do they work?"

"Well, there are nautical knots," I began. "You could use one to tie a boat to a dock or make fast a sail."

"So a knot can link things and hold them steady," he said.

"Yes, like a knot that ties a plant to a trellis and gives it the support it needs."

"Good. Keep going."

I traced a shape on the table with my finger. "I've seen jewelry, silver and gold wires, that has been twisted into shapes called love knots. I guess they symbolize the linking of two people."

I drew the shape again, as if it were dangling from a chain, then thought of the heart necklace pulling against my neck. "There are knots that can be tied and tightened until they hurt you, even kill you. Like a hangman's noose."

"Keep going."

"You can be bound and gagged, kept prisoner by knots."

"Yes. Keep going."

"Knots can be hard to untangle, so they could be a symbol of confusion. Sometimes a person will say her stomach is in knots—like before an exam."

"And what does that mean?"

"That she's anxious, scared, worried."

"Keep going."

"That's all I can think of."

Dr. Parker sat silently, chewing his sprout sandwich, sipping his tea.

"So," he said at last, "knots can be positive and negative symbols. They can represent a whole spectrum of feelings, and even those that seem opposite aren't really. For example, sometimes our ties with people support us and allow us to grow. But those same ties can restrict us, strangle us."

It was like that with my mother, I thought, but I would never tell him that. "So you're saying that Nora can be feeling any of these things and this is how she expresses it?"

"If she's the one tying the knots," he replied.

"But the strange thing is—I probably didn't make this clear—she's not always—that is, I haven't seen her—I mean sometimes things seem to move when—" I broke off.

"She's not touching them?" The psychologist picked up a honey scoop and slowly twirled the golden liquid off the stick and into his tea. "Lauren, do you know what RSPK is—recurrent spontaneous psychokinesis?"

I tried to string together the meanings of the words. "No."

"Do you know anything about poltergeists?"

"Poltergeists? I've seen the movie."

He poked the honey stick back in the jar. "Spielberg's, I assume. Well, that gives you a sense of what some poltergeist activity is like, objects moving around without being touched—sliding across the floor, flying through the air. It can also be noises, knocking, or voices calling out—some activity for which there doesn't appear to be a physical cause."

Things that move with no hands touching them, I thought. It was what my mother had described, what I had seen.

"In the movie," Dr. Parker went on, "a group of dead people were causing the commotion. In cases investigated by parapsychologists, this kind of activity has been attributed to recurrent spontaneous psychokinesis, RSPK. That is, we think it is caused by the recurring and spontaneous mental activity of a person who is alive.

"Many of the documented cases are traceable to an individual who is profoundly disturbed or under great stress. Some are children, a majority of them are adolescents. It's rare to find such ability in adults. The subject may have a history of mental problems, but not always. In any case, during a crisis of some sort, the phenomenon suddenly appears—it can be quite spooky. It disappears after the stress subsides, when the mental conflict is resolved."

"Can Nora control this thing?" I asked.

"I'm going to rephrase your question. Can the individual who is responsible control it? Some who have been studied in the laboratory can, but to a limited extent. Many are totally unaware of what they are doing. It is often an unconscious response to trauma in their lives. Do you understand what I'm saying?"

"Yes, that in a sense, Nora is telling the truth when she says someone else broke the lamp and tied the knot. She really doesn't know she's done it."

"Not exactly. What I'm saying is that if Nora is doing it, she may not know; if Holly or you are doing it, you may not know."

"But I—"

He held up a finger, interrupting me. "I haven't written down the poltergeist events you have related, but you should do that, noting who was in the area during the time each one took place. I'm suggesting you three girls because seven years ago and now, you have spanned early to late adolescence and, as far as I can tell, you have all been in the area of the activity."

"Is there a limit to the distance in which it can work? The night I saw the plants move in the greenhouse, Holly was at the prom."

"That would be stretching it," he said, "but it's possible."

"But it's got be Nora," I insisted, picking up my bottle of water, swirling it.

"She is an obvious candidate," he conceded. "But sometimes the individuals who appear the calmest on the surface don't know how to deal with their emotions and therefore express them unconsciously this way."

"So it could be Holly," I said.

"And it could be you. From what little you have told me, I gather you felt loved by your mother, but also bound by her, your freedom choked when she accompanied you to Wisteria. Those conflicting feelings could have, in a sense, tied you in knots. And returning to the scene of her death for the first time, especially after putting it off for seven years, has got to be stressful for you."

I rested my elbows on the table, my head in my hands, my fingers shielding my eyes from him. I didn't want it to be me. I didn't want Nick to be right when he said "get over it."

"I still believe it's Nora."

Dr. Parker finished the food on his plate and drained his teacup. "It could well be," he said, wiping the side of his mouth, missing the crumbs. "I have just one piece of advice. Keep an open mind, Lauren. A quick theory is a dangerous way to answer important questions."

Dr. Parker offered me a ride home, but even at midnight, Wisteria was a safe town to walk through. When I arrived at Aunt Jule's, the music was off, the torches out, and the cars gone, all but Nick's. Only Aunt Jule's sitting room light shone from the street side of the house. Since Holly was always turning off unused lights, I figured she and Nick were cleaning up on the river side.

Halfway along the path that ran between the two gardens I discovered I was wrong. Nick and Holly stood just beyond the roses, kissing. I stopped, transfixed, watching where Nick put his hands on Holly's back, studying how she put her arms around his neck. I tried to read the expression on his half-hidden face to see if this was the most spectacular kiss he'd ever had—the way his kiss had felt to me. I noticed he didn't suddenly pull back and look at Holly surprised. She was good at it, and he kept kissing her.

Her long dark hair looked gorgeous next to his blond. I saw him softly touch her hair. I felt as if I had swallowed glass, my heart cut into a million sharp pieces. Thankfully, they were too immersed in each other to notice me. Then Rocky barked.

Holly and Nick turned quickly and caught me staring. Rocky bounded toward me, his tail wagging, pleased he had spotted me. Holly smiled. Nick seemed stunned to see me and pressed his lips together. I could feel his displeasure from fifteen feet away, and I focused on Holly.

"Lauren," she said, "I was worried about you. We both were."

Both? I winced at the white lie.

"Where were you?" she asked.

"Nowhere special. I just went out for a while."

She studied my face. "Is everything okay?"

"Sure."

Holly's arm was around Nick's waist, her thumb hooked in his belt loop. "After you went in," she said, "I was afraid I had been insensitive, that I should have realized the boys were going too far. You're sure you're okay?"

"Yes."

"Where did you go?"

"To see a friend. Listen, I'm going to bed. We can clean up tomorrow."

I turned my back before she could detain me with further questions. Once inside the house I rushed through the hall and up the steps, slowing again when I reached the top to walk quietly past Aunt Jule's room.

When I reached my own, I eagerly reached for the doorknob and turned it, but the door wouldn't open. Remembering that I had let out Rocky, then locked both the porch door and this one, I pulled the old-fashioned key from my pocket and inserted it.

The door swung inward, swung into darkness. I was sure I had left on the bedside lamp. Bulbs burn out, I told myself, and flicked on the overhead light. My chest tightened. Everything was in knots—everything that I had untied before seeing Dr. Parker.

I strode across the room and checked the double doors. They were still locked from the inside. My skin prickled. No one, nothing could have gotten in, except a power that wasn't stopped by walls. I nervoulsy plucked at my bedsheets. I could untie the knots a second time, but then what? Even locked doors wouldn't keep me safe. I felt powerless to stop Nora from whatever she wanted to do to me.

I walked across the hall to the room that had been my mother's, wondering if I'd find knots there. The photos and other things pertaining to my mother had been removed by someone, but nothing else had changed. I saw Holly's door was open and checked her room from the hallway.

"Looking for something?"

I jumped at Holly's voice.

"You're awfully edgy," she observed. "Are you sure nothing's wrong?"

"Something is wrong," I admitted. "Go look in my room."

She did and I took another quick look at hers. Nothing had been disturbed.

"I don't believe this!" I heard Holly exclaim. She returned to the hall. "What is going on, Lauren? When did this happen?"

I told her about the knots that I'd found and untied earlier.

"So it's happened twice tonight?" She rubbed her arms. "That's creepy."

"Do you remember the summer my mother came, how she kept finding her scarves and jewelry knotted?"

Holly nodded. "I don't like it. I don't like it at all."

"That makes two of us," I replied.

She turned suddenly and pounded on her sister's door. "Nora!" she shouted. "Nora! I'm coming in."

Aunt Jule came hurrying from her room. "What's going on?"

"Look for yourself, Mom. Look at Lauren's room. I told you before, but you wouldn't listen to me. Nora is out of control."

Aunt Jule entered my room, and Holly opened her sister's door. Nora stood before us in a frayed nightgown. Her dark eyes darted between Holly's face and mine.

"I'm losing my patience with you," Holly said. "You're way out of bounds, Nora. Get in there and straighten up Lauren's room. And don't try something stupid like this again."

"Just a minute," Aunt Jule said, coming back into the hall. "How do you know Nora is responsible? There were lots of kids going in and out of the house tonight."

"Oh, come on, Mom," Holly replied, but then she turned to me for backup.

"I found the knots earlier," I explained, "untied them all, then locked both doors to my room. When I came back, the knots were tied again in the exact same way."

As I spoke, Nora slipped past us and entered my room. I followed her and watched from the doorway as she touched the knots in the sheets, then the knots in the curtains, fascinated by them, admiring them.

"Did you keep the key with you?" Aunt Jule asked.

I turned back to her. "Yes."

Her eyes flashed. "So why do you think Nora had a better chance of unlocking the door than anyone else?"

I glanced away. If I talked about poltergeists, I would probably lose Holly's support.

"It seems to me, Lauren, that if we want to start accusing people, you're the most likely candidate for this prank," Aunt Jule went on. "You're the one who has the key."

"But that doesn't make sense!" I protested. "Why would I mess up my own room?"

"For attention. You're a girl who is used to a lot of attention."

I saw Holly glance sideways at me; she was considering her mother's suggestion.

"I didn't do it!" I insisted.

"Someone else did it," Nora whispered, emerging from my bedroom. Her face was as white as a wax candle, her pupils dilated.

"Nora, you look ill," Aunt Jule said.

"She *is* ill!" I screamed. "And you're cruel not to get her the psychiatric help she needs!"

Aunt Jule gave me a stony look, then said in a gentle

voice, "Nora, love, I want you to sleep in my room tonight."

Nora slowly followed her down the hall.

I shook my head, amazed at how my godmother could twist things to accommodate whatever she wanted to believe.

Holly sighed. "Come on, Lauren, let's take a walk. Then I'll help you undo this mess."

"Thanks, but you've got to be tired. It won't take long to untie things."

"Still, let's walk," Holly persisted. "You're not going to fall asleep in the state you're in now."

"I'll be okay. I'll walk and talk to myself until I bore myself to sleep."

Holly laughed lightly. "Well, you know where I am if you need me."

When I reached the hall stairs, Aunt Jule stood at her bedroom door. "It's late, Lauren. Don't go far."

I answered her with a slight nod.

Downstairs, I headed out the river side of the house, then turned toward Frank's. I walked his land along the river and sat for a while in one of his lawn chairs, thinking things over. I recalled what Dr. Parker had said at the prom and knew he was right: I could do nothing about Nora's illness; the one person in my power to heal was myself. I needed to go to the place where my mother had died, this time on my own.

fifteen

The moon was high, making the unlit dock stand out clearly in the water. I imagined it as my mother would have seen it that night, a vague shape in the river mist. The bank wasn't as eroded then, so she could have climbed up easily. Had she walked the dock the way she used to walk the porch? Had someone cornered her there?

I climbed up and walked to the end where she had fallen. I forced myself to touch the piling, laying both hands on it, then stared down into the river.

Had my mother known she was going to die that night? Had she blacked out the moment she hit the piling or did she sink slowly into watery unconsciousness? Did she cry out for me?

"Get over it, Lauren," I told myself aloud. "You have to let go."

But I couldn't, not until I knew what had happened then and what was happening now.

I mulled over the poltergeist theory. Perhaps Nora was so traumatized by finding my mother drowned that she believed and feared she was still in the river. But Nora's irrational fear would make more sense if she had actually murdered her. My mother's presence had brought plenty of anger and dissension to Aunt Jule's usually quiet house. Perhaps Nora, already unbalanced—more so than any of us had realized—had been pushed over the edge and, in a sense, pushed back.

If Nora were guilty of murder and trying to repress it, my return to Wisteria would be intensely disturbing to her and could evoke a response as extreme as poltergeist activity. The puzzle pieces fit.

Then Dr. Parker's words floated back to me: *A quick theory is a dangerous way to answer important questions.* But my experiences in the last three days, some of them spookily similar to my mother's, had convinced me that her death wasn't an accident. And if Nora didn't murder her, who else could have? Who else had a reason—or the momentary passion and anger—to push my mother against the piling and off the dock? I didn't want to suspect anyone I knew; the excuse of insanity was the only way I could deal with it being Nora.

I retraced my steps, then climbed the hill and circled the house. It was completely dark now. Passing by the greenhouse, I was surprised to find that a light had been left on. I didn't remember seeing it when I arrived home and it seemed odd that Holly, given her compulsion to turn off lights, hadn't extinguished it. I entered the greenhouse, a little timidly after last night's experience.

The place felt overly warm and stuffy. I wondered if Nora had forgotten to open the vents, allowing the day's heat to build up. The bare bulb hanging over the center aisle was out; the beacon I'd seen was a large plastic flashlight. Perhaps Nora had come with it tonight, planning to cool down the place, and been frightened away by party guests.

I knew that when the sun flooded the greenhouse tomorrow the plants would die in the accumulated heat. The wheel that opened the roof vents was at the end of the main aisle, where the small trellises were. As I headed toward it, I played the flashlight's beam over the plants, listening intently, watching, afraid to blink my eyes. But every leaf was still. At the end of the aisle I shone the light on the pots with the young vines. All of them were limp, hanging from the trellises by their knots.

Above them was the six-inch metal wheel that cranked open the house's high vents—that is, the axle from it—the wheel was gone. I was sure I had seen the vents open the other day. I reached for the switch that ran the big exhaust fan, flicking it one way, then the other. It wouldn't turn on. Stranger yet, despite the breeze that night, the blades were absolutely still. When I shone the flashlight on the fan, I saw that the flap behind it had been closed, which was done only in winter to seal out the cold air. I tried the smaller fans distributed along the plant benches. They didn't work, nor did the center light.

It must be the power supply, I thought, and searched for a metal cabinet containing a circuit breaker. I found an ancient box with two screw-in fuses. Both had been removed.

Still something was running—I could hear the quiet motors. Space heaters, that's what was making it hot. The heaters burned kerosene and were used in the winter to keep the plants warm. I found four of them in the side aisles of the greenhouse and turned them off, puzzled as to why Nora or anyone else would have them running.

There was little I could do to save the plants except open the door and hope some cool air would waft in. I decided to transport at least one of each kind outside and carried a heavy pot to the entrance.

When I tried to open the door, it wouldn't budge. I set down the plant and shone the flashlight on the lock. The door had a deadbolt, the kind that required a key and could be locked from inside or out. But I hadn't locked it and the key kept on the hook next to the door was gone. Someone had taken it and turned the bolt from the outside. I couldn't believe it—I had walked straight into a trap!

Nora's trap. She must have been nearby, waiting until I was at the other end of the greenhouse to lock the door. But she was supposed to have been with Aunt Jule. Again I considered the possibility of another person being responsible for my mother's death and the things that had been happening to me. Nora's crazy behavior would provide a convenient cover, and it would be easy enough to mimic her. Who knew about the boathouse incident? Nick and Frank, Holly and Aunt Jule—and anyone in the town whom they might have told.

I tried to illuminate the area beyond the door, but the flashlight's reflection off the glass surface made it impossible to see more than a foot beyond the greenhouse. I clicked it off and stepped back from the door, retreating farther and farther into the rows of plants, hoping that as I became less visible, I would detect some movement outside.

Something touched my neck. I pulled away from a bench of plants and clumsily banged into the one across from it. It was my own sweat trickling down, nothing else. The heat was oppressive. A dull headache throbbed behind my eyes. I wanted to sleep.

The obvious way to escape was to break the glass, but I was reluctant to. The large square panes were old and might be irreplaceable. I decided to rest there till Holly or Aunt Jule woke up and found me. I sat on the damp brick floor, longing to put my head down, but something kept nagging at me. The missing fuses, the sealed fan. I pulled myself to my feet again and waves of dizziness broke over me. I felt sick, as if I had inhaled fumes, but I could smell nothing but the rich earthiness of the greenhouse.

Lack of ventilation, space heaters, sleepiness, no smell—my muddled mind kept groping for the pattern it sensed but couldn't identify. Sleepiness, no smell—carbon monoxide! The gas could be generated by heating units. It was odorless. And it could kill.

I had to break a window. I remembered that there was a hand shovel by the trellises, but I was closer to the front of the greenhouse, and the path to the back seemed long to me now, wavering in front of my eyes like a distant patch of road on a hot day. The flashlight, that would work.

I had left it on the ground when I'd sat down. I leaned over to pick it up and pitched forward. It took all of my strength to straighten up. I discovered I couldn't look down—just moving my head made me dizzy. Crouching slowly, grasping the end of a plant bench with one hand, I felt with my other for the flashlight.

My fingers curled around its plastic barrel. I pulled myself up and moved uncertainly toward the front of the greenhouse, like an old woman feeling her way along the pews of a church. The open area by the entrance would allow me to take aim at the glass from a safe distance.

I stopped where the benches ended, about six feet from the front wall, and hurled the flashlight toward a pane. But my body had become as sloppy as my mind from the poisonous gas. The flashlight glanced off the metal frame without making a crack in the glass.

Unable to walk without support, I got down on my knees and crawled to the flashlight. I knew I'd get cut, smashing the glass at close range; the best I could do was turn my face away. Kneeling close to the window, holding the flashlight like a hammer, I banged against the glass relentlessly.

Shards fell like a shower of prickly leaves, stinging my arms. I knocked the two-foot square out cleanly, then dropped the flashlight on the grass. Standing up, thrusting my head through the opening, I gulped my first breath of fresh air and felt the cold breeze on my sweaty skin. Then I blacked out.

*　　*　　*

"Lauren? Lauren?"

I opened my eyes and quickly shut them again, drawing back from the bright light shining in my face. It clicked off.

"Lauren, can you hear me?" Nick asked.

A long dog tongue licked my face. Reaching up, I put my arms around Rocky and sat up slowly. I felt sick and scared. I wished Nick would hold me and be as gentle as he was with Nora, but I wouldn't ask for his comfort. I buried my face in the dog's fur.

"Your arms are cut," Nick said. "I want to check them."

Without looking at him, I held out one, then the other, and felt him probing the skin.

"Nothing deep," he told me, "mostly scratches. Still, you should soak in a tub to make sure all the glass is out," he added, his voice sounding almost clinical. "What happened? Why did you break the window?"

"Someone was trying to kill me."

"What?"

I petted Rocky until I felt in control. "I was out walking," I said, "and saw a light on in the greenhouse, the flashlight you're holding. I went inside. It was hot and stuffy. I couldn't ventilate the place. The fuses were pulled, the fan sealed, the vent crank broken. Space heaters had been left on. When I tried to leave, I found the door locked, locked from the outside."

I gazed up at Nick's face, waiting to see the flicker of realization. Behind him, the house lights came on. Nick glanced over his shoulder, then back at me.

"Don't you understand?" I said, but I could see by

his face that he didn't. He wouldn't allow himself to believe that someone in Wisteria was a murderer.

"Understand what?"

"Nick, someone tried to kill me—to poison me with carbon monoxide!"

Another light went on downstairs, and three figures came out on the porch.

"What's going on?" Holly shouted to us. "Is everything all right?"

"Fine," Nick called back to her.

Fine, I thought wryly. Aloud I asked, "Why are you here, Nick? Did they call you?"

"Someone did," he said.

"Nick, is Lauren out there?" Holly asked. "She's not in her room."

"She's here, she's fine," Nick replied. In a quieter voice he said to me, "After I got home someone telephoned my house three times and hung up. The Caller ID listed Jule's number. I thought Nora might be upset and trying to reach me."

"She was upset," I told him, "and sleeping in Aunt Jule's room tonight—at least, she was supposed to be." I saw Holly hurrying toward us, followed by Aunt Jule and Nora. "So why did you come to the greenhouse?"

He hesitated. "It made sense to check here first. Nora spends a lot of time here."

I gazed at him doubtfully.

"And I saw the flashlight on," Nick added.

"When I used it to break the window, it was off."

"I don't think so," he replied.

"I know so."

Nick glanced away. "You're too groggy to remember anything clearly."

Holly stopped a few feet away, noticing the broken pane in the greenhouse wall and the pile of glass shimmering in the grass. Her jaw dropped. Nick stood up quickly and went to her, but I was still too dizzy to move.

Aunt Jule caught up. "Oh, no!" she exclaimed. "Lauren, are you all right?"

"Yes."

"Nick?" Aunt Jule said, turning to him. "What happened?"

He repeated his story about the phone calls, then recounted what I had told him. Aunt Jule and Holly glanced back at Nora, who was peering at me from behind them.

"Lauren seems to be all right," Nick concluded. "I saw the glass shattering, then her head come through. I lifted her all the way out. She wasn't unconscious for long. And the cuts are superficial."

Aunt Jule leaned down and reached for my hands, stretching out my arms to study them. "I don't understand. What was the point of all this?" she asked.

"To kill me," I answered bluntly. "To poison me with carbon monoxide."

She let go and took a step back. Holly looked incredulous, but then her face grew thoughtful. If there was anyone I could make understand, it was she.

"I don't believe it," Aunt Jule said. "This is the nonsense Frank planted in your head after your accident. Who would want to kill you?"

"I don't remember," Nora said softly.

"The same person who killed my mother," I answered Aunt Jule.

"Don't tell," said Nora.

Aunt Jule ignored her. "No one killed Sondra, Lauren. It was an accident."

"I used to think so." Holding on to Rocky, I rose to my feet. "So why are you all here? Who got you out of bed?"

Aunt Jule glanced at Holly.

"Nora woke us," Holly admitted. "She said something was happening outside."

"How did Nora know that?"

"She always has difficulty sleeping," Aunt Jule replied defensively.

"Yes, she had difficulty the night my mother died," I said. "I went to see Dr. Parker tonight."

Holly looked surprised. "Is *that* where you went? Oh, Lauren, you should have told me. I didn't realize you were that upset."

"We talked about the knots," I continued.

Holly glanced at Nick, and he put his arm around her. Aunt Jule and Nora listened, both of their faces pale.

"Dr. Parker said the knot-tying could be poltergeist activity."

"What?" Holly exclaimed.

"He said that most of the time the phenomenon is caused by an adolescent, someone who is very upset. It's a way of dealing with intense, suppressed emotions. Often it's not even conscious. The person doesn't know he or she is responsible."

Holly frowned and shook her head slightly.

"My mother's things were tied in knots just before she died. Tonight, my things were."

"Lauren," Holly said, "I think you need to talk to someone else. Coming back to Wisteria has been a lot harder on you than any of us thought it would be. We need to find you another counselor, one who is more—"

"It's real! It's happening!" I exploded. "Accept it!"

"It's real, it's happening," Nora echoed.

The others gazed at Nora, then me with the same concerned, tolerant expression. I would have been angered by their patronizing looks, but I didn't believe they were thinking what their faces showed. I didn't trust any of them. Not Nora, not Aunt Jule, not Nick, not Holly. They knew things they weren't telling me. Maybe they had agreed among themselves not to tell me.

"I promise you," I said, "I'm going to find out what happened to my mother and what is happening to me."

"All right," Holly answered softly, soothingly.

"Nick, I want to keep Rocky tonight."

"If it makes you feel safer," he replied with a shrug.

"It does," I said, starting toward the house. "Rocky doesn't pretend like the rest of you."

sixteen

I finally got some sleep Tuesday night, lying with my back against Rocky's, listening to his dog snores. Early the next morning I went outside with him. While he swam, I fell asleep again on the grassy bank. Holly awakened me.

"This doesn't look good," she said, smiling, "one of my party guests asleep on the lawn the morning after."

I sat up. "What time is it?"

"About nine-fifteen. How are you feeling?"

"Okay. My headache's gone and I'm not nauseated anymore."

She nodded. "I opened the greenhouse door and turned on the fans to air the place out. Did you realize there's a big exhaust fan at the back of the greenhouse? Of course," she added quickly, as if afraid she'd hurt my feelings, "it might not have helped last night."

"The exhaust fan was sealed," I told her, "as it is in winter."

"No, it's automated now. The flaps open when you turn on the fan."

"So you replaced the fuses?"

"The fuses?" she repeated. "I just hit the switch."

"Holly, there wasn't any electric power in the greenhouse last night. I couldn't turn on the fans or the light."

She bit her lip, then said quietly, "Sometimes, when people get frightened, they think they're doing something, but they're not thinking clearly so they're not doing it right."

"I was doing it right."

She didn't want to argue with me. "Well, maybe. Let's get some breakfast."

"You go ahead. I'm not hungry."

"Come on, Lauren, you'll feel better if you eat something."

I gave in and called Rocky. Nick's wet and fragrant dog made it as far as the hall entrance to the house. "Please, not on an empty stomach," Holly pleaded.

I brought Rocky's breakfast out to the porch, some of last night's meat and a piece of toast, though the toast was supposed to have been mine. Heading inside to make more, I entered through the dining room door and stopped in my tracks.

Aunt Jule's work lamp had been knocked over, its white globe broken, the fragments scattered on the table. In the basket next to it a dozen colorful embroidery threads were tied together in fantastic knots. I debated whether to call to the others. No, Aunt Jule might accuse me again of seeking attention. Let her find

it and see how it felt when this strange phenomenon
was directed at her.

I started toward the kitchen, then backtracked—
there was something amiss in what I had just seen.
While the lamp's cord was pulled from the socket, it
wasn't knotted. The cord of my bedroom lamp had
been yanked from the wall plate and knotted. The
lamp broken the day I arrived had also had a knotted
cord. Perhaps it was the process of making the knot, the
psychokinetic force used to tie the cords, that caused
the lamps to tip over, and similarly, the force exerted to
knot the swing's rope that caused it to snap. But there
was no knot in this cord. It was as if someone had
added the lamp to the scenario, overlooking that one
detail. Maybe someone *was* mimicking Nora.

But who—who would have a reason to hide behind
her behavior and wait for a chance to kill me? The
question I had asked myself at the bank two days ago
flickered in my mind again, and this time I couldn't
snuff it out. What *was* the nature of the relationship
between my mother and Aunt Jule? Had it gone bad at
the end?

My mother had died the summer she'd written the
new will, which left everything to me, with that one
provision. Aunt Jule had asked me here, knowing I was
nine months away from my eighteenth birthday and
that she would inherit the money if I died before then.
But I couldn't believe that my own godmother would
hurt me.

I wasn't naive. Life in Washington had taught me
how the desire for money destroyed the values of all

kinds of people. But while I could almost imagine that Aunt Jule only pretended affection for me—perhaps it wouldn't be hard, visiting me twice a year and seeing me now for just a few days—I couldn't believe that she would allow her own daughter to be blamed.

Still, some curious puzzle pieces fit. Perhaps Aunt Jule had been refusing to get help for Nora because she knew she would need her as a cover. If Nora were accused of murder, she would be helped rather than harmed, getting the psychiatric care she needed and eventually released. In the end Nora would share in the wealth she had "earned." Aunt Jule had always had a knack for quietly getting what she needed.

Hearing footsteps on the stairs, I continued on to the kitchen. My godmother entered a few moments after me. "Good morning, girls."

" 'Morning," we both murmured.

"How did you sleep, Lauren?"

"Okay," I answered.

"And you, Holly?"

She pulled her head out of the newspaper. "Not bad."

"Well," Aunt Jule said, "Today's a new—"

A long, plaintive whimper came from the next room. Holly quickly put down the paper.

"I didn't do it!" Nora cried. "I didn't!"

"Here we go again," Holly muttered as the three of us hurried into the dining room.

I watched Aunt Jule's face, searching for some sign that she already knew what was there. Both she and Holly noticed the lamp first, then the knotted embroidery silk.

Holly suddenly turned to me. "You don't seem very surprised, Lauren. Did you know this was here?"

"Yes," I admitted. "I saw it when I came in."

Holly frowned, silent for a moment. "I want to believe you. I really want to believe you're not playing pranks, but I just don't know what to think."

"I didn't do it!" I insisted.

"I didn't do it," Nora echoed.

"Then who did?" Aunt Jule asked, setting the lamp base upright.

Nora edged toward me. "It's a secret. Don't tell."

"Oh, shut up!" Holly said.

Aunt Jule fingered the knots, her lips pressed together.

"If someone tells, will Sondra wake up?" Nora asked. "I won't tell."

Holly whirled around and Nora winced.

"I hate this, Mom!" Holly exclaimed. "Can't you see that Nora needs help? She's making life miserable for all of us."

Aunt Jule stared coolly at Holly.

"Nora, you are so messed up!" Holly said. "You are *really* sick."

"Holly!" Aunt Jule chided.

"You're out of control, Nora," Holly went on, pacing back and forth, combing her hair with her fingers. "You need to be locked up! You belong in a lunatic—"

Suddenly Holly stopped, the color draining from her face. She yanked on her hair, then she reached back with her other hand. I saw her swallow hard. I thought at first that it was her hands flexing her hair, picking it up off her neck. I watched with disbelief as a long strand of black hair twisted itself into a knot. Then another, and another.

Holly clutched at her hair, her eyes widening with fear. She leaned over and shook her head, pulling on her hair, as if she were being swarmed by bees.

"Make it stop, Nora!" Holly screamed. "Make it stop!"

Aunt Jule stood paralyzed. Nora looked terrified.

I know what this is, I told myself; there is nothing to be afraid of. I reached for the frightened Holly, trying to steady her, then caught her hair in my hands and held it till the bizarre storm of energy had passed.

The hair fell limp, though still in tangles. Nora turned and ran out the porch door. Aunt Jule started after her.

"She's crazy, Mother," Holly said, her voice shaking. "She's psychotic. Lauren is right—that was no accident last night."

Aunt Jule looked silently at Holly, then continued after Nora.

Holly was trembling all over—with anger or fear—perhaps both. I felt bad for her but relieved for myself. Finally I wasn't alone.

"Sit down," I said gently. "Let's get you untangled."

It took a half hour to work the knots out of Holly's hair; for a few of the tangles I had to use scissors. I knew Holly was upset because she didn't say a word except *yes* each time I asked if I should cut out a knot.

Aunt Jule returned without Nora. Holly had regained her composure, but when she spoke she still sounded irritated. "I know where Nora hides. I'll find her when I'm ready."

That wasn't for another hour and a half. We cleaned up from the party, then Holly left me with the final task and went off in search of her sister.

"Where is she?" Aunt Jule asked, when Holly returned alone to the kitchen.

"I don't know. I checked all of Nora's hiding places twice. And I looked at Frank's."

"Did you call her name?"

Holly struggled to keep her temper. "No, Mom, I called out *Susie!* Let her be for a while, okay? Her behavior is outrageous. It will be good for her to think things over."

"She thinks too much already," Aunt Jule said, and retreated to the dining room.

Through the doorway I saw that a lid had been put on the basket of knots and the broken lamp cleared away. With the yard clean and the house quiet, it seemed like just a peaceful day on the Shore. But I knew all of us were waiting; it was only a matter of time before something else happened.

As I headed outside I heard Nick in the garden greeting Rocky. When he saw me, the warmth in his voice quickly disappeared. "How are you?" he asked tensely.

"Okay," I replied. "But we've had another incident."

"What kind?"

Holly emerged from the house carrying her school backpack.

"You want to explain?" I asked her, not wanting to be the only one relating bizarre events.

"You can," she said, "but he'll just defend Nora. He always has."

When I'd recounted what had happened, Nick put his arm around Holly. "Is Lauren exaggerating?"

I bit my tongue.

"No, it was just *so* freaky, Nick."

He touched her hair softly. "Are you okay?"

"Yes. Thanks."

He turned to me. "Where's Nora now?"

"We don't know. Missing, hiding."

"What happened before the incident?" he asked.

"What do you mean?"

"What did you say to Nora to set her off?"

The heat rose in my cheeks.

"Be fair, Nick," Holly interjected.

"I didn't say a word," I told him.

"You didn't bring up what happened last night?" he asked. "You didn't start talking about your mother again?"

"No!"

"Nick, Nora is crazy, as crazy as they come," Holly said.

"Maybe," he replied, "but it sure would help if Lauren forgot the past."

I looked him in the eye. "You're asking for the impossible."

"I'm asking that you think about the effect of dragging Holly, Nora, and Jule through a lot of pointless stuff. You're making it hard on all of them."

My eyes stung with tears, and I quickly blinked them away.

"Come on, Holly," he said.

She looked at me uncertainly. "Lauren?"

"Bye."

I walked back into the house. I thought I'd be relieved to hear the sound of Nick's car fade away, but it only made me ache. Why had he turned against me? There had to be more to it than the cartoon. Had someone told him something else that angered him or made him mistrust me?

I paced around the garden room, thinking about Nora. For her safety—and my own—I would feel better knowing where she was.

There was a jingling of tags, then a nose pushed in the soft screen of the porch door.

"Hey, Rocky. Wouldn't Nick take you to school?" I let him in. When I sat down, the dog rested his chin on my knee, wanting me to pet him. "Maybe you can help, old boy. How are you at retrieving people?"

He wagged his tail.

I wondered if Nora was hiding somewhere off the property. There would be plenty of places in town where she could melt into the surroundings undisturbed by others—the college campus, the docks. I decided to search for her and hurried upstairs to put on my running shoes. The phone rang and I picked it up in the hall.

"Lauren? Frank."

"Hi, Frank. What's up?"

"Holly was over here earlier, looking for Nora."

"Yes," I said quickly. "Have you seen her?"

"Just now. I was chasing an army of geese off my lawn and saw her enter the boathouse."

"The boathouse!" I exclaimed. "She's afraid of going in there."

"That's what I thought," he replied. "What worries me is that she, well—to put it mildly—looked disturbed."

"We had an incident this morning," I began.

"Holly told me about it. Is Holly there now?"

"No, she's gone to school with Nick. I'll check on Nora."

"Is Jule at home?" he asked.

"Yes. Do you want to talk to her?"

He was silent for a moment. "No," he said. "I was going to suggest that she accompany you to the boathouse, but on second thought, Jule doesn't handle Nora very well. Don't say anything to her—let's see what's going on first. I'll meet you there myself, in case you need a hand. In about five minutes?"

"Yeah, thanks."

Frank clicked off. I put the phone down slowly. Holly was sure that Nora didn't go off the property, and she was wrong. Maybe I was just as wrong about Nora's fear of the boathouse. Maybe Nora could pretend like the rest of us.

I went downstairs and called Rocky to take him outside with me.

"Who was that?" Aunt Jule asked as I passed by the dining room.

"Just Frank. I need to take some things back to him that were borrowed for the party."

She nodded and continued with her needlepoint.

Rocky followed me halfway down to the boathouse, where Frank was waiting for me, then went off for a swim.

"I'm sorry to take up your time," I told Frank.

"No problem. I thought about going in the boat-house myself," he said as we walked toward it, "but I didn't want to scare her and have her bolt again."

The door was halfway open. "Nora?" I called from the entrance. "Nora?" I thought I heard a whimper and stepped inside. "Nora, it's me, Lauren. Are you all right?"

My eyes slowly adjusted to the light. I saw a gray shape—Nora lying still on the walkway.

"Frank, something's wrong!"

I rushed to her. As I did, the boathouse door closed swiftly behind me.

seventeen

I froze. I couldn't see in the sudden darkness. "Frank?"

"Nothing personal, Lauren," he called from outside, sounding as easygoing as when he'd said, "No problem."

I heard him put the padlock on the door.

"Frank? Frank!" I shouted.

There was no reply. My mind raced, trying to comprehend the situation. Why would he do this to me? Why had he put me in here with Nora?

The thin slit between the river doors and the hairline fractures of light between weathered boards allowed me to see no more than her form. I took the last few steps toward her. If I touched Nora and she was cold—I laid my hands on her. She was warm and breathing, but unresponsive to my fingers.

People don't fall asleep naturally in places they fear, I thought. I debated which to do first, get her conscious or find a way out, then I rose quickly. If Nora awoke and went beserk, I'd be trapped in here with her.

I needed the ax, the one I had left beneath the light chain. Using my hands more than my eyes, I moved as fast as I dared on the narrow walkway, feeling my way along the wall until I touched the beaded chain. The ax was gone.

Frank knew it was here. He must have removed it— he or Nick. I was bewildered by his actions and sick at the thought that Nick could be involved, but I didn't have time to figure out the situation.

Maybe the loft would have another tool. I continued working my way to the corner of the building and along the back wall. The ladder should be soon, I thought, it should be now. I should have passed it. I touched the second corner and my heart sank. The ladder, too, had been removed.

I heard a soft moan, then Nora stirring. I held my breath.

"Mom?" she called.

If she suddenly got up and fell over the side, I'd never find her in the dark water. "Stay still, Nora. Stay where you are," I said, and began to retrace my steps.

"Mom?"

She might not become hostile if she thought I were Aunt Jule. "Yes, love. I'm here. Go back to sleep."

"Where am I?" she asked. "Is this the place for crazy people? Are you locking me up?"

I winced. "No, Nora, you're home."

"You're not Mom." Her voice sounded clearer. She would soon realize where she was.

I said nothing more until I was four feet from her. "Nora, it's Lauren."

I heard her draw back.

"Everything's okay. Just stay against the wall. Lean against it."

There wasn't a sound from her.

"Are you hurt, Nora?" I asked, moving closer to her.

She didn't answer.

I took another step and crouched down. "What happened?"

Still, she was silent.

"Do you know what happened to you? Tell me so I can help you."

"Don't tell," she whispered.

"It's all right, you can tell me."

"It's a secret."

"You can tell me the secret."

She said nothing.

I waited a few moments, then tried a different tactic. "What hurts?" I asked. "Does your stomach hurt? Your arm?"

"My head."

"Why does it hurt?"

"Because I'm crazy," she said softly.

I blinked away unexpected tears, imagining what it was like for her, trapped inside her own dark world. I felt for her fingers. "Take my hand and show me where it hurts."

She guided my fingers. When I touched the crown of her head, she cried out.

"Is it sore?" I asked. "Is it bruised?"

She whimpered.

"Did someone hit you?"

"Don't tell."

"You can tell me. It's okay."

"It's a secret."

"When did your head start to hurt?" I asked.

"I don't remember."

"Were you in a hiding place?"

She was quiet for a moment. "In Frank's garage. It hurts, my head hurts!" She whimpered like a small child.

In the distance I heard a boat motor. I hoped it was turning away from us and wouldn't create a wake. "Did Frank find you in his garage?"

She continued to cry.

I laid my hand cautiously on her back, then rubbed it, trying to soothe her. The boat engine sounded closer. "Is the garage one of your hiding places, Nora?"

"Yes."

Then either Holly or Frank could have found her there. After her hair was knotted, Holly was scared and angry. Had she lost her temper? No, it was Frank who had lured me here, and most likely it was he who had struck Nora.

I heard the boat zip past us. So did Nora—I could feel her body get rigid. "Where am I?"

"You're okay."

She heard the watery movement and her voice quivered. "I'm in the boathouse. Sondra is here."

"It's not Sondra. It's just a wake."

As soon as I said a *wake*, I realized my mistake. I

quickly rephrased it. "It's the waves from a boat, a passing boat." I wondered if that was how these imaginings had started—someone saying it was "a wake" and Nora, haunted by the death of my mother, twisting the words in her mind.

She was shaking. I reached for her hands and felt the fear in her as she grasped mine with icy fingers. I wrapped my arms around her and held her tightly. The waves slapped against the outside of the building and rocked the water inside. But the motion of the water lessened quickly, the series of waves ending sooner than it had the last time.

And then it started, just as it had before, the slow rocking of the water back and forth, back and forth—sideways, I realized. The direction of the flow was wrong—it couldn't be a wake.

"She's here," Nora said, her voice low and terrified. "She wants you. She wants her little girl."

The water slapped hard against the walls. Nora's arms wrapped around me, her fingers grasping my shirt, twisting it so hard I felt her knuckles digging into me. I braced myself, trying to keep myself from being pushed into the water. I felt her shifting her position, but before I could react and throw my weight against the wall, she did. She held me against it, as if protecting me.

At last the water grew quieter and settled into a dark restlessness.

"You're okay," Nora said. "She didn't get you. I didn't let her have you."

A lump formed in my throat. She had tried to keep me from being "taken" by my dead mother.

"Nora," I said. "Do you know how the knots happen?"

"I don't try to do them."

"Someone else does?"

"Someone else inside me. I can't stop her. Only sometimes."

Her unconscious, I thought. Sometimes she could control the emotions giving rise to the poltergeist, sometimes she couldn't.

"Listen, I think I know how this water gets stirred up. There's a lot of stuff in here, things we threw in the water years ago. There are old ropes and nets, especially around the doors, where we used to fish. I think this person inside of you gets angry or afraid and moves those things, whips them around and ties them in knots. That's what stirs up the water."

"No, it's Sondra," she insisted.

"Remember how the lamp in the river room broke?" I continued. "When that person inside you got upset, she tied the knot in the cord, which yanked on the lamp and made it tip over. The same thing happened to the lamp in my room. And the swing—with my weight at one end and the tree anchoring it at the other, it had to snap when it was forced into a knot."

The heart necklace, too, I thought; it had risen against my neck because it was being tied.

"Nora, we just have to talk to that person inside you, and tell her that everything is all right. It's not Sondra. Sondra isn't here."

"But she is," Nora insisted. "Holly said so."

I sat back on my heels. Holly, who said she alone

knew how to handle Nora—perhaps she alone knew how to torture her. I wanted to blame Frank, Frank entirely. But as I went over the various incidents in my head, I could see how easy it would be for Holly to hide behind Nora's behavior. I reluctantly took the plunge. "Why did Holly hit you?"

"I didn't tell, I didn't!" Nora pleaded, like a child who had been suspected of telling a secret and threatened with punishment.

"Didn't tell what?"

She wouldn't answer.

"What did Holly hit you with?"

"I don't remember."

She might not, I reasoned, if she were hit on the back of the head. "Do you remember what Holly was carrying when she found you in the garage?"

"The lamp."

"The lamp that was broken? Your mother's work lamp?"

Nora nodded yes. "My head hurts," she whimpered. "Inside and outside it hurts."

The mental pain was probably worse than the physical, and I hated to cause more, but if I didn't know what had occurred and who the enemy was, I couldn't help either of us.

"How did she hold it?" I asked, wondering if Holly was simply dumping the lamp in Frank's trash or using it as a weapon.

"With a glove, my garden glove."

My breath caught in my throat. She'd wear a glove if it were a weapon and she didn't want her fingerprints on it. But why use something as traceable as a brass lamp—why not a block of wood that could float away in the river? Holly was too good at details and planning—something wasn't right.

I rested my hand on Nora's. "You and Holly have a secret," I said. "Holly thinks you told the secret. Now that she thinks you have told, you can."

I waited for a response, struggling to be patient.

"The secret is about the night my mother died," I ventured.

Nora didn't reply, but I took this as a positive sign. She said no quickly when she wanted to deny something.

"You came to my room that night," I went on, "looking for Bunny, your stuffed animal. You had left him on the dock. I said I would get him for you, but you said you could go as far as the dock. You left the house, and then what?"

She slipped her hand from beneath mine. In the dim light I saw her pull up her knees. She hugged them tightly.

"It's okay. I just want to know what happened next. Were you alone?" I changed the question to a statement. "You were alone."

"No. Holly was there, she was coming in."

"Coming in as you went out?"

I remembered then, running down from the house to the dock, stepping on something sharp, waving Holly on—she was in her nightgown but wearing shoes.

"Did you say anything to Holly? Did she say anything to you?"

"I don't remember."

"I know you do," I replied gently. "Did you tell her about Bunny?"

"Yes. I started getting scared about going out on the dock. I asked her to get him."

"And she said?" I laid my hand on Nora's arm and felt the tension in her muscles.

"She said I couldn't be afraid of water and I'd have to get him myself."

"And then?"

"I wanted her to come with me while I got him, but she said no."

"So you got Bunny yourself? Where was he?"

"On the dock. He was all the way at the end. I had to go all the way to the end."

I could hear the fear rising in her voice.

"It's okay. We're just remembering now. It's not happening now. Did you pick up Bunny?"

"Yes."

"Were you alone?"

"No."

I held my breath.

"Sondra was in the water," Nora said. "When I picked him up, I saw her floating in the water."

I sagged back against the wall. My mother had fallen in before Nora arrived.

"I killed her."

"*You* killed her!" I exclaimed, then softened my voice. "Did you push her? I thought she was already in the water."

"I didn't get her out. Holly said I should have pulled

her out. Holly said I knew how to swim. I killed Sondra when I didn't pull her out. But I was too afraid. I knew I should go in, but the water was dark and scary. I thought the river wanted me, too. I rang the bell."

"Nora, listen to me. You didn't kill my mother. It wasn't your fault. You rang the bell. That was a good thing to do."

Clutching her legs, pressing her forehead against her knees, Nora rocked herself. "Holly said she wouldn't tell anyone I killed Sondra if I promised I wouldn't tell anyone I saw her outside. *It's a secret,* she said, *don't tell.*"

I bit my lip, bit back my anger at Holly. She could be innocent, I argued with myself; she could have been nothing more than scared. She was only eleven at the time. Perhaps she had set up Nora in case she herself were falsely accused, guilty of nothing more than looking out for herself at the expense of someone else. But she had used Nora cruelly, and today she had hit her, left her, and lied to Aunt Jule and me—at least to me.

Nora began to cry. "Holly said you were coming back to Wisteria because you were angry about your mother's death. She told me not to talk to you and said that you would hurt me if you knew."

"She was wrong. I'm not going to hurt you, Nora."

Nora sobbed loudly.

"And you must believe me—you didn't kill my mother."

The sobs grew uncontrollable.

"You didn't. I swear to you!"

Were Frank and Holly working together? What

about Nick? I shrank from the thought that he was involved, but he was Frank's nephew and Holly's boyfriend, the link between them.

"Nora, why would Frank lock me in here? Do you know?"

Her sobbing grew less as she thought. "To help me?" she guessed.

I doubted it. What puzzled me was the fact that Frank didn't disguise his effort to trap me. No one would believe what crazy Nora might say, but why wouldn't Frank worry about an accusation by me?

The answer stopped my breath, shrank my stomach into a cold, hard rock. He wouldn't worry if I were dead. He planned to kill me.

He—or they—were setting up Nora, beginning to work on her mentally by trapping us together. My death would be hung around her neck. It wouldn't be hard; she had shown herself confused enough to accept the guilt for my mother's.

I pulled away slowly from Nora. "I have to get us out of here. I'm going to look for a tool."

I walked all the way around the boathouse, feeling for something I could use to smash the hinges of the door. The place had been stripped clean.

"Okay, Nora, I'm on the other side now. Don't get scared. I'm going to scream for help."

I shouted till I tasted blood in my throat. It was useless. Who would come—Aunt Jule? She couldn't hear from the house. Besides, she could be part of the plan.

She'd have to be if my inheritance were the goal, and that was the only motivation for murder that I could imagine. Frank, as lawyer and executor of the estate, would be able to process the will as quickly as possible, using his local clout to pull strings if necessary. But Aunt Jule was the designated heir, so there would have to be some agreement between them. As for the tension between my godmother and Frank, partners can quarrel, especially when the stakes are high.

I heard movement outside. I screamed again. Nora started shrieking with me. I hurried around the walkway to her. There was barking.

"Rocky!" I shouted. "Rocky, get help."

Rocky, get help? What did I think he would do—run off like a dog in a Disney movie and fetch the police? I started laughing and crying at the same time, getting hysterical.

I heard noises at the back wall of the building, Rocky barking, Frank telling him to keep quiet. The noise stopped. I heard Frank leave, his voice fading as he called the dog.

I removed my shoes. "Nora, there's only one way out of here, under the doors to the river. I'm going to swim under and go for help."

I put my feet over the side of the walkway, then rolled on my stomach so I could slide into the black water.

"No," Nora protested. "No, don't!"

"I'll be back."

"She's in there. She'll get you."

Nora pulled on my arms. I was stronger than she and slipped free of her grasp, then thrust myself back in the water. When I straightened my legs and pointed my toes, they barely brushed the silty bottom. I tread water, trying to keep my mouth above it. Its slimy surface coated my arms and neck. Its earthy, sulfurous odor filled my nose and seemed to seep through the pores of my skin.

I turned my head, sniffing something different from river and rot.

"Nora, do you smell smoke?"

I heard her taking in deep, soblike breaths. "Yes."

For a moment I was so shocked I couldn't think what to do. It was too horrible—I could not believe that Frank would set the building on fire with us inside.

"Nora, get in. You have to get in the water."

I heard her pull back against the wall.

"The boathouse is going to burn down. We have to get out of here now. Now! There's no time. You must come with me."

"No!"

"I'll help you. I'll hold on to you."

"No!" she shrieked.

It was useless to try to convince her. She wasn't thinking fire, she was too afraid of water.

"Okay, never mind," I said quickly, and grasped the edge of the walkway. "Help me get out."

As soon as her arms were around me, I pulled her into the water. She screamed.

"I'm here. Float on your back. I'll help you."

But she was terrified. I fought to get her into a lifesaving carry. She clawed at me and tried to climb up on my shoulders. Desperate to get herself above the water, she pushed me under.

I struggled to the surface. Her fingernails dug into my skin. She was much stronger than I'd realized and pushed me down again. I dropped way down, pulling Nora with me, hoping she would panic and let go.

It worked. I swam three feet away from her, then came up for air.

The smell of smoke was strong, smoke and lighter fluid. My eyes stung with it. Nora was treading water but was so frightened she kept gulping it down.

"Get on your back, Nora."

Her arms flailed wildly toward me, and I propelled myself backward in the water, out of her reach. She went under.

I dived and searched frantically for her, then grabbed her and pulled her to the surface, wrestling her onto her back. Out of the corner of my eye I saw a bright flame shoot up a corner on the land side of the boathouse. I heard the crackling. Another flame shot up the second corner, as if following a trail of lighter fluid. I thought I heard barking, but it was too late to hope Rocky would draw attention. Doused with an accelerant, the wood in this house could go up in a matter of seconds.

I swam, dragging Nora toward the river doors, then stopped in front of them. She was coughing and I had to make sure she had air.

"Come on, Nora. Deep breath in, deep breath out. Deep breath in, deep breath out. That's the way. Deep breath in—"

I sucked down my own lungful of air, then pulled her under with me. I swam toward the light, one arm keeping her next to me, kicking hard for both of us. In the murky water I didn't see the net, didn't know I had swum into it, until it was around us. I pulled back quickly, trying to find its edge.

I had to let go of Nora for a moment. Using both hands I yanked on the netting in front of me, tearing at it with my fingers and teeth, making a hole just big enough for one of us. I swam through it, then reached back and pulled Nora to me.

Almost there, I thought, my lungs burning for lack of air. I took Nora's hand and curled her fingers around the waistband of my shorts, wanting her to hold on to me so I could use both arms to swim. Suddenly I felt her let go. She bolted like a frightened animal, driven by her instincts, swimming directly upward. I saw the net, but she didn't. She was caught in it—a new net—a plastic one, one that wouldn't tear.

Nora clawed at it, pulling it around her even more, getting hopelessly tangled inside. I tried to pull it off her. She writhed, desperate for air. My own lungs ached, my body began to cramp.

I felt the net twisting, being wrenched away from me, and I lost my grip on her. I spun in the water till I was sick and didn't know which way was up.

Then suddenly there was clear light around me. The air was cold against my face, and I opened my mouth and drank it down. Strong arms held my head just above the water. I gulped and coughed, bringing up river water and a bitter fluid from my stomach.

"Easy. Easy now."

It was Nick's voice. Nick's arms. He turned me on my back and swam with me, pulling me to the bank. I heard Rocky barking. Sirens wailed, were getting louder, coming closer.

I tried to speak. *Nora,* I wanted to tell him, *get Nora!*

I felt other hands take me from Nick. I reached back, but they carried me away from him and the water.

"Two hundred feet!" a woman shouted. "Get her away. Go!"

I was finally laid down in the grass. I tried to sit up. Everything slid past me, out of focus, the world running with water, smelling of river and fire. "Nora! Find Nora!"

Someone crouched next to me. An arm wrapped around my back, supporting me. "She's safe," Nick said. "She's just a few feet away."

I reached out, trying to touch Nora, wanting to make certain she was there.

Nick caught my fingers. "The police are taking care of her," he assured me. "Paramedics are on the way."

I leaned back against him and rested my cheek on his shoulder. I could feel the river water dripping off him.

"Thank you," I whispered. When I looked up, I saw he was crying.

eighteen

I asked to speak with the sheriff privately. I had left Nora sitting up, fully alert, and very frightened. It had taken the effort of both Nick and me to loosen her grip on my hand and wrap it around his. Aunt Jule was talking to the medics. The boathouse smoldered—what remained of it—and volunteer firefighters continued to work. McManus, the man who had questioned me about the rock-throwing incident, told another officer to take charge and walked with me toward the house.

"So," said the sheriff, sitting on the edge of the porch, pulling out a worn notebook, "I asked yesterday if there was anyone you weren't getting along with these days. Want to try a different answer?"

"It's a long one," I warned him, then recounted everything that had happened, including events from seven years ago, ignoring the strange look I got when I told him about the knots. I mentioned the will without telling him why it worried me. If desire for my mother's money was a reasonable motive, he would see it, I told myself. The truth was, now that I was safe, I didn't want to believe it. It hurt too much.

"I don't have any physical evidence against Frank," I concluded. "It's what I say against what he says."

"And Holly?"

I hesitated. "Like I said before, she could have been scared and protecting herself the night my mother died. The spooky stuff that's happened—I think that was all Nora. I think Holly hit Nora today, but she may have lost her temper without having any idea what it would lead to. I—I just don't know."

The light-haired sheriff pushed his hat back and forth, as if he were scratching his head with it. "Frank's not here. We checked next door—that's policy with fire. The house is locked up and his car gone. I've already talked to Nick and Jule."

"What did Aunt Jule tell you?"

He ignored my question. "They're fetching Holly now. And Nick's parents—I like a kid's parents to be around for these things. Why don't we just sit back and see what Holly has to say, without bringing up what you've told me?"

"So she doesn't shape her story around mine?" I replied. "Is that why you aren't telling me what Aunt Jule said?"

He smiled. "That wouldn't be too smart of me, now, would it?"

"What if we pretend Nora died?" I asked. "If we tell Holly that I found Nora unconscious and that Nora died in the fire, she'll think I know nothing at all about what happened earlier today or the night my mother died. There would be more chances of—" I stopped myself.

"Catching her in a lie?" he prompted.

Was that how little I trusted her now? "Or showing that she is honest," I replied.

Twenty minutes later we gathered in the garden room. While I was changing into dry clothes, McManus had told Aunt Jule and Nick about our plan and had instructed them not to contradict him. I felt guilty for setting up Holly and kept telling myself I was giving her the chance to demonstrate her innocence, but when I entered the garden room, I couldn't meet Nick's or Aunt Jule's eyes.

Holly had just come from the boathouse, her face looking pale and damp. "Are you all right, Lauren?" she asked.

"Yes," I answered, stepping back quickly when she reached for me, not wanting her to touch me.

She turned to Aunt Jule. "Now maybe you'll believe that Nora is out of control. I blame you for what has happened, Mother, all of it."

Without saying a word, Aunt Jule retreated to the river room. Both sets of doors were open between that room and the garden room, and I watched her pace.

Holly walked over to Nick and took his hand. Seating herself close to one of the porch doors, she drew Nick into the chair next to hers. Though the doors were open, both sets of drapes that covered them had been closed halfway. Nora was on the porch outside with a police officer, so she could listen.

I sat opposite Holly and Nick, and the sheriff squatted on the hassock between them and me. He stared at his notebook for several moments, then removed his hat.

"Holly, I have some difficult news to give you. Your sister didn't make it."

Holly blinked. "What?"

"Nora died. You know that she and Lauren were trapped in the boathouse."

"Yes, a firefighter told me, but—"

"Lauren found Nora unconscious. She swam under the doors to get help, but the fire had started, and the place went up like a matchbox."

"Oh, God," Holly said. "Oh, God, why?" She turned to me. "How did this happen?"

I told her about the phone call, finding Nora unconscious, then the door being padlocked by Frank. A warning look from McManus silenced me before I said more.

Holly's eyes filled with tears. "Where's Frank now?" she asked.

"We're looking for him," McManus replied. "He's not home. Not at his office. It's starting to look like he's nowhere in town."

Holly frowned. "Why would he do this?"

"That's what we're trying to figure out," the sheriff told her. "Do you have any theories?"

"No. No, how could I?" Holly said. "It's horrible! I can't even imagine it."

I wanted to end this miserable charade. "Sheriff—" I began.

He cut me off. "I have some theories of my own and would be interested in any ideas or observations you have, Holly. Sometimes little things you notice can go a long way toward giving the big picture."

"Things like what?" Holly asked.

"A statement someone made that gave you reason to pause. An argument you overheard. Anything that can help us piece this together."

Holly stared at the floor, biting her lip, then looked up slowly. "Mother?"

Aunt Jule stopped pacing and came to stand in the doorway.

"Mother, what have you told them?"

"What do you mean?" Aunt Jule asked.

"I want to know what you have said to the police."

"The little I know," she replied, stepping into the room. "I was home. I heard Rocky barking, but didn't pay attention. Then I heard the sirens."

There was a long silence.

"Holly, do you believe there is someone else involved other than Frank?" McManus asked. "Have you seen or heard anything to make you think that?"

"No—maybe," she said indecisively.

"I'd like to hear about that *maybe*."

Holly wrung her hands. "This is . . . really unpleasant." She looked down at her hands and made them still. "I think that Nora wasn't the one somebody was after."

McManus leaned forward.

"I think it was Lauren my mother wanted dead."

Aunt Jule's face went white. "What are you talking about?" she exclaimed.

Holly kept her eyes on McManus. "Before Lauren's mother drowned, she wrote a will with the help of Frank. She left everything to Lauren, but if Lauren died before she was eighteen, everything would go to my mother."

"Holly, what are you saying?" Aunt Jule cried. She leaned on the wooden back of a chair, her arm rigid, the rest of her body sagging against it. "Do you think I would hurt Lauren? Do you think I would hurt anyone for money?"

Holly straightened her shoulders, steeling herself. "If her name was Sondra or Lauren—yes. I think that you killed Sondra first."

"I did not!"

"You fought with her constantly that summer," Holly said, her voice becoming stronger in response to her mother's denial. "The night she drowned, the arguing was awful." She turned to me. "Do you remember?"

I saw the curtains move and for a moment was afraid Nora would reply, but she remained quiet.

I looked from Holly to Aunt Jule, not sure whom to believe. Each seemed shocked by what the other had said. Then suddenly the piece that didn't fit, one tiny observation, slipped into place. Why would a person who planned as well as Holly use a traceable object to strike Nora? Because the lamp was Aunt Jule's and would have her fingerprints on it. What if it wasn't Nora who was to be framed for my death, but Aunt Jule, who had the most obvious motivation?

"Yes, there was a lot of fighting," I admitted, "but I

know your mother wouldn't have hurt my mother or me. And I can't believe she'd ever hurt Nora. I won't believe it," I added, "not without some kind of evidence—stains or fingerprints."

"Did you look for the weapon?" Holly asked McManus.

"What weapon is that?" he asked.

"I thought that Nora was struck—" Holly stopped midsentence.

She had been too quick to point the investigation in the direction of the lamp, too eager for the sheriff to follow the plan she'd laid out for him.

When she didn't go on, McManus said, "I told you that Lauren found Nora unconscious. I didn't say how she got that way. She could have fainted, could have been poisoned."

I saw the curtain move again, its long cord swinging loose.

"She could have," Holly agreed. "But I figured it happened the way it does on TV."

The cord swung as if in a breeze. Nick turned his head slightly. Aunt Jule noticed it. But McManus's eyes were on Holly, and hers on him.

"I'm not a detective," Holly went on. "I'm not trained to think of all the possibilities. Like Lauren, I can't believe my mother would do this. It—it horrifies me. It doesn't seem real."

The cord swung like a pendulum, closer and closer to Holly's right arm.

"And Frank—he's like an uncle to me. I trusted him! I trusted both of them."

"Holly," Aunt Jule cried, "why are you turning on me?"

The tip of the cord curled upward as if invisible fingers had twisted it.

"You've got it backward, Mother," Holly argued. "*You* turned on us. My sister is dead. And if I don't say what I know, Lauren may be next."

Tears ran down Aunt Jule's cheeks.

Holly's face hardened. "Stop faking it, Mother. Who else would want to kill Lauren?"

The moving cord suddenly twisted upward and snaked around Holly's wrist. It coiled twice and knotted itself, tying Holly's forearm to the wooden arm of the chair.

McManus rose from his seat, his notebook sliding from his lap. "Good God!"

Holly sat still and appeared perfectly calm, but her arms prickled with goose flesh.

There was a long ripping sound. The curtains on the other door fell and the cord flew across the room. It twined itself around her wrist. Holly's skin paled, her eyes widened with fear. She struggled to get free of the rope, rocking back and forth in her chair, knocking into the glass door. "Stop it, Nora!" she screamed. "Stop it!"

Two officers stepped into the room.

"Move aside, Nick," McManus said.

Holly's eyes darted over the room, as if she expected Nora to come back from the dead.

"Nora, you can come in now," McManus called.

Holly wrenched around in her chair and stared at Nora as she came through the door, then she turned to me. "Witch," she said, with unnerving calm.

I didn't reply. I had no answer for the hate in her eyes.

"You're such a fool, Lauren," Holly said. "Did you really think that anything had changed between us during the last seven years?"

"I hoped we had both grown up."

"You will always be rich and stupid, just like your mother," Holly said. "You don't deserve what you have. You don't deserve your money and you don't deserve my mother's sickening admiration. I have always hated you."

"Enough to attempt murder?" McManus asked.

She ignored him. "I told Frank you were an idiot and would be easy to take in. You trusted him like a puppy dog."

"I guess I am naive," I answered. "I never imagined that you could hate me so much you'd make your mother and sister suffer for it."

"Who doesn't help me, hurts me," she replied coolly. "They stood in the way."

"Of the inheritance?" McManus asked. "Perhaps, Holly, you figured that if both Lauren and Nora were dead, and your mother charged with double murder, the money would be yours. At least, you'd be given control over it."

"You're smarter than the rest of them," she said.

"Of course," McManus continued, "it would help to have Frank moving things along legally. What was he supposed to get out of this?"

"My mother's property for a good price." She sounded proud—she sounded absurd, as if there were no difference between a murder plan and a yearbook layout.

"The boathouse was Frank's idea," Holly went on. "He saw it was in his best interest to help out. I knew Frank was in bad financial shape—he leaves his papers all over his home office, like he thinks a teenager can't read. He's got several banks and some real unhappy investors breathing down his neck. He was desperate to have something to offer them.

"I want a deal," she told the sheriff. "I'll give you the evidence you need on Frank, but I want a lawyer with brains to represent me and a good deal from you."

"We'll talk about it back at the station," McManus replied.

Holly eyed Nora. "You let me down, Nora," she said bitterly. "You screwed your own sister."

Nora stepped behind me, as if needing my protection.

"I am the one who let you down," Aunt Jule said, "all three of you. It's way past time that I tell you why I asked Lauren to come back to Wisteria.

"Seventeen years ago, when Sondra came here pregnant and terribly upset, I myself was pregnant for the third time. Sondra lost her child. Her baby is buried next to her in the churchyard."

That was the grave I had seen, the one I'd thought was mine.

"Meanwhile, I had a child I couldn't afford. We agreed that it would be best for all three children if Sondra took Lauren and pretended she was hers. I knew that Lauren would receive all that a child could want and that Sondra would love her dearly. Sondra sent money every month to help support us here. As part of the agreement, my little girl was to visit each summer.

"But as Lauren grew older and Sondra more troubled, Sondra and I began to fight about how Lauren was being raised. When they came that last summer and I saw how painfully confused Lauren was by Sondra's behavior, I was furious. We fought about Lauren day and night, as you all well know.

"It's hard not to be overly critical and jealous of the woman raising your child. But I loved Sondra. I did not kill her. Still, I knew Nora had problems and feared that she had. I was afraid that in therapy, that secret would be discovered and they would take Nora away from us. I thought if I could keep her safe here at home, everything would be all right.

"I knew I had to tell Lauren the truth about her birth, but the longer I put it off, the harder it was. When I finally made up my mind to do it, and Lauren came, painful memories were stirred up in Nora. I worried that Nora might hurt Lauren and was afraid to explain the past and make things worse. I didn't know what to do."

Aunt Jule gazed at Nora and me, then turned to Holly. "I have not been a good mother. I have made terrible mistakes. But I have always loved you." Her voice wavered with emotion. "I will never stop loving all three of you."

I wanted to put my arms around Aunt Jule, to reassure her, but I couldn't. I struggled to comprehend that she was my birth mother and to reinterpret all the things I had thought I knew about myself. Nick, who was standing a distance behind us, came forward and took Aunt Jule's hand.

I finally found my voice. "Nora is innocent of my mother's—Sondra's—death," I said. "Holly convinced Nora that she was guilty because she didn't go into the river to pull her out, but Nora wasn't responsible."

Aunt Jule closed her eyes and shook her head.

"Okay," McManus said, "I think this soap opera's over, at least for now. I'll be sending someone back to you folks for some more statements."

An officer cut the curtain cords around Holly's wrists. When Holly stood up, Aunt Jule tried to put her arms around her, but Holly pushed her aside. "I hate you! I hate all of you."

"I want cuffs on her," McManus said.

"Traitor," Holly hissed at Nick, then moved toward me. Two officers moved with her.

"Excuse me," she said, "I have something private to tell Lauren."

They looked at me and I nodded.

She took a step forward and whispered in my ear, "I killed Sondra, but you'll never be able to prove it." Then she turned away laughing and was escorted out the door.

nineteen

As the police exited, Nick's parents arrived. They said a quick hello to Aunt Jule and rushed over to Nick. I don't know how the three of them understood each other, for they all talked at the same time. I turned to Aunt Jule—in my mind, that was still her name. I hugged her and Nora, then pulled away, feeling suddenly shy.

My godmother—mother—touched my cheek gently. "It's okay, love," she said. "It's going to take a while to get used to the idea.

"Your dad knows," she added, "he has since you were three. I didn't realize Sondra had told him, not until we spoke at her funeral. The loss of Sondra had upset you so badly, we both thought it best not to tell you about your birth until you were older. Whenever I visited you, your dad would call to find out how I thought you were doing. He may not have been an ideal father—he certainly wasn't a good husband to Sondra—but he does love you."

I nodded silently. There was so much to absorb.

Aunt Jule hugged Nora and smiled at me, as if to send me the hug vicariously, while giving me the space I needed at the moment.

"Do you want one of your walks alone?" she asked. "See, I'm learning that you're not a little girl anymore and like to work things through by yourself."

I smiled back at her. "Yes, but I want to take Rocky with me. Tell Nick I've got him, okay?"

The dog trotted next to me down to the boathouse. I kept a tight hold on his collar as we watched the firefighters continue to douse the grass around the burned-out structure. Fishing line, crab traps, and nets, some of which looked new, had been dragged out of the water. Yellow police tape surrounded the site.

"Come on, Rocky," I said and headed in the direction of the dock. He raced past me, then plunged into the water. I watched him swim and tried not to think about Nick.

I had discovered that there was something more painful than falling in love with someone who hasn't fallen for you: hurting that person—hurting him and not being able to do anything about it. I wondered if Nick suspected that Holly had killed my mother. I wouldn't tell him. Holly was just a kid then—maybe a heartless one, but a kid, and legally a minor. If I pursued the matter I'd create more pain, not achieve justice. I told myself it was Holly and Frank who had betrayed Nick; still, my return to Wisteria had triggered the whole disturbing chain of events. I wondered if Nick and I would ever be friends again. I thought about the way he had cried when he held me on the grass.

Think about something else, I told myself, think

about Dad. In nine months I'd inherit my mother's money and wouldn't be dependent on him anymore. It would give me a better chance to strengthen our fragile relationship, to let him know I didn't need, but *wanted*, his presence in my life.

And the money would enable me to pay for the psychological care of Nora—for the care of my sister, I thought, trying out the new words. I'd stay the summer and, if she needed me, do my senior year in Wisteria.

"It's going to get better," I said aloud.

"It will."

I turned, startled by Nick's voice. He stood a foot away from me.

"Didn't mean to scare you," he said. "Can we talk?"

"Nick, I'm so sorry. I know how much it must—"

He reached out and touched my mouth with the tips of his fingers. "What I meant was—can *I* talk?"

"Okay."

We walked together, following the riverbank. After a long silence he said, "I'm trying to put it all in order."

"Don't try. Just begin anywhere."

"Do you know what it was like kissing Holly and looking up to see you?"

"What?"

"You said to begin anywhere."

But I hadn't expected that as a beginning, middle, or end. I felt my cheeks getting warm. "I guess it was pretty embarrassing for both of us," I said, and walked ahead of him so he wouldn't see my face. "I know, I just kept staring at you."

"What were you thinking?"

"I don't remember."

"Don't *you* start using that line," he chided.

"Then don't ask me, Nick." Did he suspect how I felt?

He caught me and turned me around to face him. I focused on his shirt.

"Okay," he said quietly, "I'll tell you what I was thinking. I couldn't believe that I, who was never going to get hooked, had fallen in love with a girl who didn't want to date, and she was watching me kiss somebody else."

I glanced up.

"Your turn, brave girl. What were you thinking?"

"That Holly looked beautiful in your arms and that you didn't pull away from her the way you had pulled away from me when I kissed you."

He drew me to him. "I'm not pulling away again," he said, holding me close.

I hesitated, then put my arms around him. "I thought I had done something stupid."

"No, you just surprised the heck out of me. I knew before then I was getting hooked on you, but I thought I could handle it. I didn't know a simple kiss could be like that. It was scary, what I felt. My heart was banging against my ribs. I don't know how you didn't hear it."

"I couldn't hear it over mine."

He tilted his head back to smile at me. "I love looking in your eyes," he said. Then the smiled disappeared and his face grew serious. "I found out right after that what *really* scary was—someone hurting you, someone trying to kill you."

"You mean today."

"No. I was suspicious before. I didn't think that Nora would hurt you, but I had begun to worry that some-one was hiding behind her. The night of the prom I real-ized how jealous Holly was of you. When I returned to the dance—I don't know, I must have had a dazed look on my face—she knew something had happened between us. She started cutting you down, saying a lot of nasty stuff. No big deal, I told myself, girls and guys get jealous of each other."

"I was sure jealous of her," I said.

"Were you?" he asked, his eyes shining. "You don't mind if I enjoy that, do you?"

"I feel responsible," I told him, "as if all of Holly's life I've gotten the attention she wanted."

"Everyone wants attention, Lauren, and everyone gets jealous. But you didn't try to get rid of her, did you?"

"No."

He let me go, then put an arm over my shoulder and started to walk with me.

"The day after the prom you told me about the note that had been left in your car. I could explain it as an anonymous prank, but as I did, I remembered that Holly had left school for a few minutes right after you. It would have been easy for her to put the note in your car while you were in the cemetery.

"And the brick that was thrown at your car, I could explain that, too, but again Holly had gone out during the time it happened. She said she had been at Frank's picking up some party things. Afterward, Frank pressed me for details about how you were getting along with Holly, Jule, and Nora. He must have realized then that someone wanted to get you."

"I—I just don't understand Frank," I said. "I knew he loved money and thought you should love it, too. I knew he enjoyed using his clout as a lawyer and businessman, but I didn't think he'd hurt people. I didn't think he'd hurt me."

"Me neither. Maybe Aunt Margaret's family was right about him. It's scary to think how easy it is to be fooled."

"I feel so bad for you and your parents, Nick. Frank is family for you; for me, Holly is. And I don't know how anyone writes off family."

"Yeah," he said, "I think Nora will have a lot of company in the next few months. You and I, Jule and my parents, we'll all be sitting in Dr. Parker's office, trying to understand what happened."

I stopped walking and wrapped my arms tightly around him. "You know, I *can* hear your heart."

"Could you hear it breaking when I accused you of getting my cartoon pulled?" he asked.

I held my head back so I could look him directly in the eye. "I didn't pull it."

"You couldn't have," he replied, "because I did."

"You?"

"I was worried about your safety," he explained, "but I thought if I accused Holly, she would deny everything. The only way I knew to protect you was to stick close to Holly and try to anticipate her next move. After the prom, I had to convince her in a dramatic way that I had turned on you. The cartoon was the only excuse I could think of."

I dropped my head, resting my forehead against his chest.

"I'm sorry, Lauren. When I accused you, I saw how badly I was hurting you. At the party I noticed Holly talking to Jason. Not long after that he and his friends started harassing you. I couldn't break it up, not without making Holly suspicious, so I sent Rocky into the water. It was the best I could do."

I smiled up at him. "It worked."

"I saw Holly enter the greenhouse twice during the party and wondered what she was doing. After I left that night, I parked in Frank's driveway and waited a while before sneaking back to investigate. I arrived just as you smashed the window."

"So there were no phone calls to your house?"

"No. You remember my stupid excuse about why I'd come to the greenhouse—the flashlight, which, as you pointed out, wasn't on."

"When you lied like that, I was afraid that you were part of it."

"You looked so betrayed—it was awful," he said. "When I left the second time that night, I was terrified at what might happen to you and went directly to the police. I talked to McManus's deputy. He drove by the house, but everything was quiet. He promised that someone would talk to you the next day, but he wasn't as worried as I. You hadn't asked for their help, and there had been a big party. Pranks happen.

"Anyway, this morning, when I learned about the

knots and the fact that Nora was missing, I knew the situation was critical. I blamed you in front of Holly to make sure I was in solid with her. After we arrived at school, I made up a sudden errand. I called the police, talked to McManus, and rushed back here to talk to you. He, another officer, and I arrived at the same time. Rocky was barking and we smelled smoke. The woman officer and I ran to the boathouse, and McManus called for backup and fire equipment. You know the rest."

"I thought you had turned against me," I said, "and all the time you were trying to protect me."

We had reached the end of Aunt Jule's property and turned back.

Rocky emerged from the river and came galloping toward us. Stopping in front of us, he shook water all over. I backed into Nick.

"Good dog," Nick said. "That's one of the tricks I've taught him, shaking water on girls so they back into my arms."

"Really! How smart of Rocky—and you, of course."

"That's another thing I've been wanting to tell you," he said, turning me to face him. "I'm tired of getting jealous of my dog. I mean, he has nice eyes, but so do I."

I looked from Rocky's golden eyes to Nick's laughing green ones.

"I didn't enjoy the way Rocky got to stick close to you while I played Holly's boyfriend. He's going to have some competition from now on."

"Oh, yeah? Are you good at retrieving sticks?"

"I'm good at stealing kisses," Nick said, then proved it.

about the author

A former high school and college teacher with a Ph.D. in English literature from the University of Rochester, ELIZABETH CHANDLER now writes full time and enjoys visiting schools to talk about the process of creating books. She has written numerous picture books for children under her real name, Mary Claire Helldorfer, as well as romances for teens under her pen name, Elizabeth Chandler. Her romance novels include *Hot Summer Nights, Love Happens, At First Sight, I Do,* and the romance-mystery trilogy *Kissed by an Angel,* published by Archway Paperbacks.

When not writing, Mary Claire enjoys biking, gardening, watching sports, and daydreaming. She has been a die-hard Oriole fan since she was a kid and a daydreamer for just as long. Mary Claire lives in Blatimore with her husband, Bob, and their cat, Puck.

DARK SECRETS™
by Elizabeth Chandler

Who is Megan? She's about to find out....

#1: Legacy of Lies

Megan thought she knew who she was.

Until she came to Grandmother's house.

Until she met Matt, who angered and attracted her as no boy ever had before.

Then she began having dreams again, of a life she never lived, a love she never knew...a secret that threatened to drive her to the grave.

Home is where the horror is....

#2: Don't Tell

Lauren is coming home, eight years after her mother's mysterious drowning. They said it was an accident. But the tabloids screamed murder. Aunt Jule was her only refuge, the beloved second mother she's returning to see. But first Lauren stops at Wisteria's annual street festival and meets Nick, a tease, a flirt, and a childhood playmate.

The day is almost perfect—until she realizes she's being watched.

A series of nasty "accidents" makes Lauren realize someone wants her dead.

And this time there's no place to run....

Archway Paperbacks
Published by Pocket Books

Jeff Gottesfeld and Cherie Bennett's

MIRROR IMAGE

When does a dream become a nightmare?
Find out in MIRROR IMAGE as a teenage girl
finds a glittering meteorite, places it under her pillow,
and awakens to discover that her greatest wish
has come true…

STRANGER IN THE MIRROR

Is gorgeous as great as it looks?

RICH GIRL IN THE MIRROR

Watch out what you wish for…

STAR IN THE MIRROR

Sometimes it's fun to play the part
of someone you're not
…until real life takes center stage.

FLIRT IN THE MIRROR

… From tongue-tied girl to the ultimate flirt queen.

From Archway Paperbacks

Published by Pocket Books

2312